DESTINY'S PLAY

SMITA RAO

ISBN 979-8-89475-394-2

TABLE OF CONTENTS

FOREWORD

Every journalist dreams of writing, as do those with a natural flair for storytelling. Inspired by RK Narayan, I, too, embarked on writing short stories. My first book received a modest reception, igniting a strong desire to further my writing career. India's vastness provides ample material for short stories, yet our linguistic divisions prompt reflection: are they a blessing or a curse? They have undoubtedly fostered distinct linguistic communities.

Today, young people transcend linguistic and religious boundaries to find love and marry across cultural divides, a trend on the rise. Consequently, India has become a melting pot of diverse religions, cultures, and castes. However, the older generation remains steadfast in their adherence to traditional values and customs. For society to achieve true peace and harmony, they must be willing to adapt and embrace change.

ACKNOWLEDGEMENT

My special thanks to each and everyone in this endeavour of publishing my second book. My daughter Suchitra, my grandson Artham, Suraj, Saloni and my granddaughter-in-law Tejal, my whole family came together to help in my efforts to publish my second book. My heartfelt thanks to Sandhya & Sudhir Mahendale for spending their precious time whenever I needed them. I thank my society people who are the first people to buy my book and show their love and encouragement. Thanks to all, Smita Rao.

TRAGEDY IN LIFE

Shivkumar Sharma walked back from his shop a worried expression itched on his face. He could not shake off the concern as he thought of the notices that had been posted on the street corner board. Two or three houses have been targeted. The stark words reading "vacate the place within two days or face the consequences." Those cruel words sent a shiver down his spine.

Your ancestral house where your people lived for generations has to be vacated within two days, if you do not obey, then the bodies hanging on the pole next to the street corner board was a witness for the consequences.

Suddenly his gaze fell on the board, No.22 that is his house number. He couldn't walk further, his legs became weak. Holding on to a roadside tree, he stood still for a few minutes. His whole body was shaking. His mind in a turmoil. Then suddenly realization dawned on him.

He had to act fast. Only two days left. Earlier he had ordered a big replenishment of his stock in view of incoming Id celebration. Then he thought nothing is more important than the life of him and his wife. His two children were studying in Bangalore his son in an Engineering College and his daughter in a Dental college. He had to plan everything very fast. Time is short. His children can be informed later.

Next day, he consulted the concerned office, how he can be accommodated in a refugee camp. Shivkumar Sharma had decided to settle in Bombay. Bombay the city of dream.

He told his wife to pack a set of two clothes. Next day he went to his shop in Gulmarg and contacted all his business associates and informed them of the tragic event. He took whatever cash available and booked a train ticket to Bombay. By evening everything was ready. Shivkumar Sharma was a meticulous person. As instructed by the usurper the house was kept open. It was three days journey to Bombay. They reached Mumbai late in the evening. The refugee camp where he was allotted a barrack was in Chembur. He took a budget hotel for the night.

Next day he met the concerned officer and he was given possession of a barrack in the Sindhi camp. It was a refugee camp. Most of them from Sindh and Kashmir. After settling in the camp he started meeting people for his job. Some of his old friends from Kashmir were also there. They were of great help. He got a job as a manager in a construction company. The salary was good. "God had been kind to me" thought Shivkumar.

He informed his children about the good news and also requested them not to come to Mumbai immediately as travelling costs a lot. They have to concentrate on their studies because that was their last year. Shivkumar's wife Seema had lot of jewellary, so it helped them in their time of crisis, his children's education completed without any hitch.

His children Arun and Sudha were twins. Sudha who was studying Dentistry in Bangalore fell in love with a boy who was studying medicine hails from a Kashmiri Pandit family. His parents were settled in Bangalore. The marriage was celebrated in Sri Sri Ravi Shankar's Ashram in a simple way with the blessings of both families. After their education, they both went and settled in Canada.

Shivkumar's son Arun was very obedient, cool and hard working. He joined his father in running the business.

Shivkumar brought the business to great heights. The old man Ravi Shastri whose business Shivkumar was running now got some ideas, if his son comes back to India, he can easily manage the business with the help of Shivkumar. He called his son and the son Ravi came to India. He had neither the ambition nor the inclination to do business. He told his father in simple words that he is not interested in the business. He is happy in Canada in his present job. Then a lump sum amount was decided in lieu of the business and a monthly annuity of a fixed sum was to be given to Mr. Ravi till his death. An agreement was signed and everything was amicably settled.

Now Shivkumar was relaxed all his worries about losing the business got settled. He wanted to go to Kashmir for a holiday. But meanwhile he got a chance to get a prime plot of land in a decent locality in Chembur. He brought the land and started building a house. He meticulously made arrangements, the house to be built in 3 parts, the ground floor for himself and his wife, 1st floor for his son Arun and his family and lastly the 2nd floor for his daughter Sudha and her family. The house got completed. Sudha got an invitation for the house warming ceremony. Sudha came with her family, her husband Anil, her son Piyush and daughter Prandyna. The whole family together took short holidays and enjoyed life. That was his best period in Shiv Kumar's life.

Sudha went back to Canada. Now the daily routine started. Year's passed leisurely. Now Sudha's daughter was in college. She fell in love with a Merchant Navy Officer, who was not a Kashmiri Pandit but a nice boy from a decent family. The marriage was fixed and celebrated in India in a grand style. One month passed in a jiffy Sudha and her family went back to Canada.

When next time Sudha visited India, she raised the question of division of property and business. Shivkumar told her he had already made provision in his property, i.e. his house for all of them.

What about your business papa "I want an equal share in the business". "The business belongs to both me and Arun". He had left his executive job and put his soul for this business. I am still healthy and want to work some more years.Then I will make a will.

"Papa life is short, we cannot predict anything. You please make clear everything now only.

I said no said Shivkumar. His voice was in a pitch. He was very angry. Sudha did not stop her arguments. What about the business asked Sudha emphatically? Why the business belongs to me and Arun. Arun has put his whole life in this business and after my death; it will be passed onto him.

"No Papa,things are not fair. The business was built by you, Arun only helped you. I want an equal share in it"

Shivkumar was shocked. How can Sudha be so greedy? She is not ready to consider Arun's sacrifice." This is really unfair" thought Shivkumar. He just collapsed on the sofa. A doctor was called and he said it is a minor heart attack. The matter was closed for the time being. Sudha went back to Canada, but before she departed she told her father "I want an equal share in your house and business. Otherwise I will severe all relations with you. Consider this not as a threat, but I am serious about this.

Shivkumar felt defeated in life. He was not so much agitated when he left his ancestral house in Kashmir. That time he was young and confident of building a new life. Now he has become old and haggard. His wife is on the early stage of Alzheimer. But still she managed the house with the help of hired people.

Shivkumar's health deteriorated for a few days. He was in hospital. He died in the hospital without making a Will. That was the crux of the matter. He never wanted to make a Will dividing his business as demanded by his daughter.

His wife was a soft spoken. Kind lady the whole responsibility fell on her slender shoulders. She was not in a position to make a Will. So the sister and brother went to court. Shiv Kumar's love for his children stopped him from making a Will. But now both are fighting in court for a solution with no immediate result. It may drag on for years.

- o 0 o -

OLD WAYS, NEW WAYS

Yenkappa had two sons. Tejappa and Sundarappa. Yenkappa was a big landlord. His eldest son Sundarappawas a rebellion son. His second son Tejappa was obedient from the very beginning. Sunderfought with his father and removed his family symbol Appa from hisname. I will be called only Sunder. He was a good looking boy. Both the sons had their formal education in their family funded primary school.Tejappafinished his primary school and became the village pramukh. Sunder went toa nearby town to study further and stayed with a distant relatives, a lawyer and finished his high school education.

Both the sons were brought up with equal care and affection. Sunder was a health freak. He used to walk 5 km every day. Their village Vasupura was a princly

Kingdom once. The hill where the school building stood today was a palace once Mr. Sunder was a loner. We used to wander on the vicinity of the school building many a times. Once he went for a walk on a road leading to a nearby village. There he saw a new Bungalow and near the gate stood a beautiful girl about his age tall, fair, slim and beautiful. He was so impressed by her elegance and regal bearings. He went a few meters and took a U turn in his track. But when he returned the lady was not there. She had returned to her house. Disappointed he returned. Everyday Sunder used to go and he wanted to have a glimpse of the girl. Once or twice he saw her. But she was so engrossed in talking to her gardener. Once their eyes met and he felt mesmerized. She had delicate features and a gentleness shown on her face. He could not gather enough courage to talk to her he made enquiries and came to know that her father is a preacher, her mother is dead and she stays with her father.

Village people loved the family. The whole family talked so sweetly, helped them in their time of need. The girl's name was Veena. She helped the poor children in their studies without any remuneration One fellow Sheena was in a financially bad shape. They helped him start a bakery and a small patch of land was given, where a dilapidated structure was there which was repaired and Sheena was settled there. Sheena converted to their faith without even their pressurizing him. Another family Ramu was also given a plot of land and a weaving machine to make Panchas. His daughter Sumati was studying in 8th class and will go for teacher's training. They were little bit coached into converting to their religion. But there was no force. So things were going smoothly for the preacher. His daughter was extra point in the game.

The news that Sunder's visits to the preacher's house also reached Venkappa. He was little worried about his rebellions son. In the meantime his sister daughter who was at the marriageable age liked Sunder very much. According to their family tradition, sister had the 1st right to give her daughter in marriage to her brother's son. The proposal came. Uma was her name. She was fair, gaunt with a hawk like nose. Sunder detested her. His father was putting pressure on Sunder. She was the sole owner of a big chunk of property. Sunder blankly refused the proposal. The whole household was shaken Sunder's father gave him ultimatum. Either marry her or leave the house. That was the last weapon. Sunder did not budge. He said he will convert to Christianity rather marry that ugly hawk. He was thrown out of the house. He went to the preacher and was advised about his right to his share of the property which he will get if he goes to court. Sunder was prepared to go to any lengthy to avoid the marriage. After a prolonged court battle Sunder won the case and he got his share of the property.

The preacher helped him financially and emotionally throughout the ensuing battle. He helped him set up a tile factory in his village and got his daughter married to him after converting him to his religion.

After the marriage, the preacher was driven out of the village. He went to Udupi and settled there. Sunder went to a nearby town and settled there. Sunder's son Raja had a soft corner for his village people. He helped the villagers to set up a high school in the village. He used to help the poor children of the village in their financial crisis. The tile factory got expanded and many local people got jobs in the factory, Village prospered. But village people still hated the preacher for converting one of their top coveted son to their religion.

- o O o -

WAITING FOR A MIRACLE

The girl was very pretty. Her mother Shasha hails from Southern India. Her husband Ratnakar was a Hotelier. On the 12th day when the baby was named Uma based on the calculations of the horoscope Shasha was not happy. It was a old fashioned name so Shasha thought Kushi was the proper name, which brought happiness to all of them.

She had a caesarian delivery. She vowed never to have another baby. Her husband Ratnakar wanted a son. But he kept quiet. Aishwarya Rai from South was reigning Bollywood. Kushi's mother nursed an ambition on her daughter to become an actress. Kushi was brought up with so much love and care. She was sent to a prestigious school in a chauffeur driver car. But Ratnakar wanted her to become doctor. But her mother secretly nursed an ambition that her daughter to become a film star. So Kushi grew up between two thoughts. After graduation, she decided to go to America to get trained in an academy, training people to become actors.

In two years, her father had spent a lot of money. She came back to India with a resolve to join film industry. She came back with lots of hope. But alas if wishes were horses. Kushi was a basically a shy person. Moreover, she was raised in the traditional and protective values of the middle class. She tried her best to get some modeling role. But she was unable to get adjusted to the atmosphere of the industry. The hard reality of the film industry hit her very hard. Here everybody tried to take advantage of a new person only sons and daughters of film`s established actors were spared of the initial ordeals and exploitation of the industry.

Kushi in spite of her best efforts could not get even a modeling assignment, leave aside a heroin's role. Every day she used to visit one or two studios. But without any result, one day her father gave her an ultimatum. You either find some work or I will find a groom for you. Kushi was not prepared to compromise on her values to become a model or an actor.

Ratnakar found a boy from their community a doctor an eye specialist. He was a good looking person, post graduate in Ophthalmology and from a good family. More than anything, he works and settled in Bombay.

Kushi has no reason to refuse the alliance. There was no reason for Kushi to disagree on the issue. It was a hard decision.

Everyone said Kushi was lucky to get such a fantastic proposed. Kushi told her father, she wanted to have a free talk with her beau before she decides toagree for the marriage. She still craved for her name tobe seen on the roadside hoardings

During their talk Kushi put the condition that in case she get some good roles, Shekhar should not object to her continuing in the industry. Shekhar know she could not survive in the cut throat style of the film industry. Engagement was announced. Kushi was looking respledent in a Manish Malhotra ensemble and the groom equally good. Everyone said "what a made for each other Jodi".

Shekhar was soft spoken, kind and understanding; when suddenly Kushi's engagement was announced, she got a role as a heroin in a T.V.serial. The marriage was postponed. Shekhar was not happy. He was in a noble profession where there was a lot of respect.

Shekhar tried to convince Kushi after the serial would wind up to get married. Kushi was in a different world. The chamak, damak of Bollywood made her very selfish and arrogant. She never wanted to give up her coveted position so easily. IT was so tantalizing. Her photos in every magazine and the fame gone into her head. She started avoiding Shekhar and his phone calls.Shekhar was a very decent person. One day he called Kushi and returned her engagement ring. She pleaded with him "Please give me some more time once I achieve my goal of becoming a heroin in a picture, I will leave erything and join you in Matrimony.

Shekhar knew Kushi is gaining time. He said OK only six months, I will not wait for you any further. Kushi was very happy. ON an impulse she hugged Shekhar. He got struck by her sudden action. He kept quiet and went back without another word. Kushi got an offer as a heroin in one film. Her T.V. role was appreciated by the audience. The film dragged on for two years. Shekhar as promised sent back her engagement ring and married a doctor whom he knew as a colleague for many years.

After the failure of the picture, Kushi did not get any new offer. She was sitting at home hoping to get some new offer. But there was none. In the meantime she came to know Shekhar got married. She had no reason to blame him. Shekhar was magnanimous enough to give her sufficient time. Such a good proposal had slipped from her hand she can blame only herself for the failure.

Many proposals came. But she could not find any suitable groom. Her mother's fear that Kushi will remain a spinster for life was coming true. Till now neither Kushi got any role or a groom, to her satisfaction. So she is waiting and waiting for some miracle to happen.

- o 0 o -

DIVINE JUSTICE

"Mummy, bye. I will phone you as soon as I get my results," Suvarna called out as she hurried towards the station. She was in her final year of Electrical Engineering at a college in V.T. She got into the ladies' compartment of the slow train to V.T., her daily routine. About an hour later, the phone rang, and her mother, Lata, received the good news that Suvarna had passed with first-class honors.

Suvarna was waiting for her friend Diksha on the platform at Masjid Station. She was continuously on her phone, pacing back and forth. Unknowingly, she reached the far end of the platform. A fast train was approaching, and within a second, she was caught between the train and the platform. A heart-wrenching cry echoed through the station. One moment, a life bubbling with joy and happiness was nipped in the bud by the cruel hands of destiny. She was gone in an instant, without pain or much suffering.

The train came to a halt. People gathered to see what had happened. Some pulled her blood-soaked body from the gap. Her handbag was lying a few feet away from the scene. The railway police retrieved the bag and found her address.

The body was sent for post-mortem. Her parents were informed of her death. Her father and mother came to V.T. Station. Within hours, her body was brought back. It was a simple procedure and did not take much time. In the morning, she had gone to receive her results; now, her lifeless body was brought back. Her mother became hysterical, crying uncontrollably, while her father shed silent tears, remorse clearly written on his face.

Why such a cruel fate? An innocent, bubbly girl died within seconds, while her parents were condemned to a life of sorrow and heartbreak. That was the punishment God had bestowed on them for their ill deeds. It was divine justice.

The story goes back to when Suvarna was a kid. Gurunath Shinde was a sweeper in the municipality in Bhandup. He had three sons. They all joined the local Shiv Sena and became prominent members. The first son, Rahul, joined the ruling party and became a significant party member. He got a job in a big company and became a union leader. The second son married a Tamilian girl and was thrown out of the house. The third son, Alok, was not much educated and became the leader of a chain-snatching gang. Suvarna was his only daughter.

It was a slow train. It stopped at Kanjur Marg for a minute. Mr. Jayant Kulkarni got down and went towards a kiosk to have a puff of his cigarette. His wife's gaze followed him. She was sitting by the window when suddenly a hand reached for her throat, pulling her thick gold mangal sutra. The force was so strong that it cut her neck, causing blood to ooze out. Her cries of pain were loud. Mr. Jayant, who was near the kiosk, saw the unfolding drama and came running. The train had started to gain momentum.

Instead of getting back on the train, Jayant concentrated on the thief, running after him. There was a kutcha road from the railway station to the main road, a heavy industrial area with several big and small factories. A small patch of land was vacant, but as the election neared, overnight, a lot of hutments sprang up. The ruling party, not wanting to disturb the vote bank, allowed them to stay, and they became permanent structures. One big factory had a high compound wall.

Jayant saw the chain snatcher hand over the chain to another fellow waiting on the other side of the factory wall. The fellow, after getting the chain, ran to the gate and vanished onto the main road. Jayant knew pursuing the thief was useless, so he returned to the platform and waited for another train. As soon as it came, he boarded and started his homeward journey.

Jayant made it a routine to get down at Kanjur Marg station to get a glimpse of the thief. But luck never favored him.

About six months later, Jayant saw a repeat of the scene. This time, the victim was an unknown lady, and he had a clear view of the thief. He ran after him, shouting, "Thief, thief!" But nobody came to his help.

There were a lot of small workshops on the left side of the road, doing machine work for big factories like Gabriel, Crompton, and Larsen & Toubro. After crossing these workshops, there was a small open land opposite the factory. Next to it, there was a chawl. The thief entered a room in the chawl. Jayant saw another fellow waiting in the room, which had a backdoor. Thefellow threw the chain to the other guy, who then ran towards the main road, crowded with vehicles and people.

Jayant caught the thief by the collar and asked, "Where is the chain?"

"What chain? I was returning from work, and this is my house. You can search it if you want, but if the chain is not found, you will face dire consequences." Suddenly, he became dramatic and started shouting.

"This fellow is accusing me of theft! You all know I am a law-abiding citizen. I will not tolerate his accusations!"

Jayant realized he would be in danger if he stayed there. He got scared and hurriedly returned to the station. For a long time afterward, Jayant never got down at Kanjur Marg.

One day, there was a big crowd on the platform at Kanjur Marg Station. People were heading towards the chawl. Jayant followed them. What he saw frightened him. An ambulance had arrived and lowered the body of a young girl. It was Suvarna, whom everyone had seen many times playing badminton there. Her mother's hysterical cries echoed far and wide. She was the daughter of the chain snatcher, Alok. Jayant saw the body, and silent tears flowed down his cheeks.

The question arose in his mind: why was Suvarna destined for such a brutal death? An innocent young girl, and on the day her results were out. Everyone present had tears in their eyes. What wrong had she done? Why such a cruel death? This question haunts every person. I have read many scriptures, the Gita many times, but the answer was not clear. Why? Why? This question kept haunting me. Today, after witnessing Suvarna's death, the answer came to me. Suvarna, a pure soul, died instantly without much pain or suffering. But her parents were destined to a life of sorrow and heartbreak for the rest of their lives. The answer is simple: what you sow, you reap. Do good deeds and get back good results in life. Don't harm anybody intentionally. The answer is multidimensional, and each person interprets it according to their own perception.

The mantra is simple: Don't harm anyone for any reason.

- o 0 o -

THE REVENGE

The whole village, woke up to hear the news priya's father Mr. Manjunath, the freedom fighter was arrested alongwith other Satyagrahis. They were all kept in a dilapidated building used as a makeshift prison for the Satyagrahis. Gandhiji's Ahimsha Andolan was in full swing.

Manjunath's wife and his children started crying. His eldest daughter Priya was a little sensible "Appa will be released soon. The Britisher's cannot afford to feed so many people for a long time.

Mr. Manjunath was a landlord. He used to get good income from his farm located in a village about 15 km from his present residence. His mother was managing the farm earlier. Now she has become old and came to stay with her son. Mr. Manjunath never was interested in farming or any work related to the farm. He used to go to the farm after the monsoon to assess to amount of rice he could get in each harvest. Slowly the yields have become less and less. The farmers were grumbling. They had to spend for the seeds, Labour manure plus the hard work they had to put in.

Once enraged Mr. Manjunath took some hired goons and went to collect the yield. The villagers came together in a group and driven the goons away from the village.

Now Mr. Manjunath realised he had to find some alternative source of income. One big plot attached to their present residence was lying idle. All of them started concentrating on developing the land. Fruit trees like Mango, Jack fruit, coconut, cashew, chicku, Jamun were planted on the periphery the middle portion was developed as a vegetable garden. The garden provided enough vegetables for their whole family. Some rice was still coming from the farm. Only cash was a major hurdle.

Priya's mummy was a teacher in the primary school teaching cutting, stitching to the girls. She was stitching clothes for the village women, earning some extra income.

Priya's father was nicknamed "well-dressed man" in the village. He wore fine Manchester Dhoti, from

England, a Mukhmulli Kurta from Lucknow and gold rimmed spectacles. He never did hard work, for that matter any work.Earlier he used to bring readymade dresses packed in card board boxes and foot wear for his children from Madras where he used to go for his court cases. It was all a luxury in those days. Mr. Manjunath would throw a party for his friends at the week end. It was a lavish lifestyle in those days. Overnight it all changed.

After his release, Mr. Manjunath brought many charkas and the whole family started weaving threads from the raw cotton from the local market. His Manchester Dhoti was replaced by a Mundu woven by the local weavers and a Jabba from the same crude cloth. In this changed circumstances, Mr. Manjunath was arrested along with other Satyagrahis and released after being detained for two days. The household heaved a sigh of relief.

At this juncture, Priya completed her 8th standard. There was no high school in the village, but Priya wanted to study further. One day her one rich aunt came visiting them. She agreed to provide afternoon lunch to Priya during her schooling years. Priya travelling a distance of 6 km every day, started her high school education.

On one Sunday Priya stayed back at her aunt's place. Her one uncle was staying a little away from her Aunt's place. She paid a casual visit to her uncle in the morning. She saw her uncle's neighbours making garlands from the loose mogra flowers, brought from the local wholesale market. She was fascinated on seeing the process.

Priya was a sweet, pretty girl interested in anything which caught her fancy. She wanted to learn the art. The weaver's family consisted of the father a Rickshaw Driver his wife a housewife, a son working in a Government office and two daughters Uma and Rama. Uma was of Priya's age and they became friends. Priya started visiting them to learn the art. Within a few days Priya mastered the art. A few days later Uma asked Priya to weave her mala. Priya was so engrossed in the work, suddenly she looked up to see the time. She saw Uma's elder brother Kartik was looking at her unabashedly. She felt so awkward, she ran from the place.. What she saw surprised her. Kartik was tall grotesque little hunch backed and the face like a cat. Priya detested anything ugly. Kartik was very ugly. She vowed never to meet him again. But destiny brought them face to face many times.

After Priya's exams, one evening she was sitting idle at home in her village. They were surprised to see her uncle coming to their place. He rarely visited them. He told Priya's mother the message Kartik had asked him to convey. There is a vacancy in the Magistrate's court for a copywriter post. Once a day, selected person would have to go to three offices.

One Magistrate's court, one collector's office and last Munsif's court for 2 hours each a total of six hours a day. Priya refused saying she has no interest in going and working in three offices. Priya's mummy asked her not to miss the opportunity to work in a government office, a secured job. Priya reluctantly agreed.

On 1st of March, she joined the service and one morning, she went to the Magistrate's office to work. ON that day, a case of a bicycle thief was going on. She was made to sit very near to the witness box. She saw from the corner of her eye, the bicycle thief looked ferocious. After the lunch break the case continued. Now she grew little bold. She looked at the thief and this time she found him an ordinary person. After that she went to the collector's office and Munsif court.

Three months passed very fast. An advertisement appeared in the local gazette for the post of L.D. Clerks for various government offices. There was no gender bias. Priya thought of applying. Kartik helped her in the process. She applied, appeared and passed the exam.

Election duty was compulsory for government employees. Priya was allotted plum postings, incharge of a complete ladies booth even though she was a junior and with no previous experience. Kartik was using his influence to promote her.

Then one fine day, Priya's uncle came to Priya's house with a marriage proposal from Karthik. "What a proposal, Rikshawala's son. Our land is gone. We have become poor. That does not mean anybody can ask for Priya's hand. What about our prestige! "Land is gone, only Lord is remained "Said Manjunath's mother sarcastically".

"Let us not fight over this. Let Priya take the decision". Her mother said slowly. Priya was sitting quietly. "No never. I will not marry him." With an emphasis on no, she surprised everybody. So the matter was closed.

Priya was busy with her work. She had to learn a lot. Slow and steady wins the race. So Priya slowly picked up. She joined the old students association of her school. She joined the ladies group for the improvement of the girls. She immersed herself in social work. Some more years passed. Neither Karthik's attitude towards Priya nor her attitude towards Karthik changed. Both were getting good proposals. Karthik realised waiting for Priya will not help him further. He got a good proposal for his sister Uma. She was little on the darker side and not much educated. A proposal from a graduate teacher in lieu Karthik had to marry the teacher's sister. It was a satte proposal. Karthik loved his family specially Uma. She he agreed for the proposal. Karthik waited many years for Priya. She never relented. So marriage was fixed. An invitation was sent to Priya also. The venue of the marriage was 20 km away. She was obliged to Karthik in many ways". So she attended the marriage.

It was late evening when all the festivities were over. Karthik requested Priya not to go alone at that late hour. He said "my friend Salman will accompany you. Priya was not happy. Then she thought instead of going alone Salman can accompany her. Salman reached her safely to her house.

The very next day a rumour was circulated that Priya was in love with Salman and they are tying the knot soon. Priya was shocked. Salman was a casual acquaintance of both Karthik and Priya. Karthik purposely had done this to spoil the name and respect of Priya. Priya was liked by everyone for her amiable nature and exemplary character. Priya realised this is sort of revenge Karthik has taken for his unrequited love

Somehow she explained to her inner circle of friends the real facts. So the news slowly subsided. The news had reached her village also. Her people knew Karthik had done this to avenge his rejection.

On one evening, she was going to her village; she met her primary school teacher who stood by her on occasions thick and thin. He directly asked her about the rumours. Priya realised the damage done by the rumours. She explained to him about the origin of the rumours. To some extent, further spreading of the news was stopped by her teacher in the village.

A few more years passed Priya married a boy, an Engineer from her own community. Priya was able to keep her respect and love from all concerned by her exemplary conduct. Even the Magistrate attended her marriage as a deviation from his normal protocol.

- o 0 o -

EXCHANGE OF BRIDES

The marriage Pandal was decorated. The rituals have started. Panditji called the girl's mother to bring the bride to the Mandap. Some ladies went inside to the dressing room where the girl was getting dressed up, to bring her to the Mandap. She was not found in the dressing room. A search party was formed and went to all corners of the hall to search the girl. The girl was nowhere to be found. One lady said "the girl had ran away. Nowadays the girls are becoming more demanding irrespective of their looks and status they wanted a boy, who is educated more likely in a Government post and smart. The groom was not so smart. He was of average height ordinary looks and a mechanic in a A/C servicing company. He studied upto 10th standard with 8 to 10 thousand salary in a month.

The girl who ran away, studied upto 12th standard, she can order dresses from Myntra, was thinking herself very smart, had a boyfriend who is a clerk in a Government office.

All the ladies gathered and started discussing who is interested in getting their daughter married to a readymade groom. The groom's family prestige in society was at stake.

Ramcharan was a migrant from Bihar. His family had migrated from Bihar. They have settled in Gaziabad in U.P. for a long time. Some people said "he is a low caste person from Bihar, that is why he migrated to U.P. But he was an outsider by all standings of their social norms.

He had three daughters. The first daughter refused the alliance. The second one was short, plump and little dumb. So Ramcharan's wife offered the hand of her second daughter Veena, after consultation with her husband. The boys side had no option. Any girl who is ready to marry their son was welcome.

Veena got dressed up with whatever was left from the bride's suitcase and brought to the Mandap. It was a ill-fitting dress and she was very uncomfortable. She was a kind hearted person looking at the pathetic condition of the groom, She felt pity for him. She vowed to make her marriage a success. His name was Laxman.

A common name in U.P. Every third person in U.P. is either Ram or Laxman. He was working in Bombay. She was exited to go to Bombay, the dream city. Marriage was performed with full Vedic rites and Veena went to her husband's house the same evening.

They all heaved a sigh of relief. So much money and the prestige of the boy's family was at stake. Marriage was over and they got a girl who was obedient and kind. Veena was very scared when she was pushed into a semi lit room in the night. Her younger sister accompanied her as is the custom. That night she was sitting on a mat with a thin bed sheet spread on it. She sat in a far corner of the mat. The boy also was equally nervous. He said "thank you for agreeing to marry me". I felt pity for you" That is O.K. "Now listen to me. Tomorrow we are going to your father's place for farferi". Ask him to provide a cot for us. Seema just shook her head. Where are you living in Bombay.

"I have no place of my own. I stay with 6 other boys of our village and share the common room. We have to go to a common toilet.

Veena heard him with utmost sincerity. "What will you do where I come to Bombay". "I will try to find a room in a chawl". "What is your salary". "Rs.8,000/- I will do some overtime and earn some extra money".

Veena was silent. The grim reality hit her hard. Whatever be the circumstances, she will make her marriage a success. Next day they made a decision whatever fate bestows on them will be endured willingly.

After a week's stay, they booked a ticket to Bombay and landed in Chembur. He got a job as a watchman in a construction company. A Tin sheet covered single room was available for the watchman. Construction water was available for 24 hours. There was a nearby common toilet in the vicinity. So Veena started her life with necessary things and a foldable cot brought from her father's place. In native place the ladies never worked as maids. Each and every one had a small patch of land which provided them necessary vegetables and rice for their daily need. Her father was a small contractor. So life was easy.

Veena got pregnant and went to her native place for delivery. She got a boy. She came back after 3 months. Then Laxman found a room and they shifted to the rented one room in a chawl. Veena was finding it difficult to meet both ends with her husband's salary. So she started working as a maid in a nearby building. She was getting good money. The next two years, she got two daughters and in the municipal hospital doctor told her to get operated on the 3rd time delivery. So she got operated.

Veena had to bear the brunt of running the family. From the beginning, her only aim was to make her son an IAS officer. All her efforts and endeavor was to make him pass the exam. All her half starved days humiliations were at the alter of her son's education.

One of the ladies where she was working was a social worker. Veena asked her to spare some time to teach her son Maths and English. The lady was a kind hearted person. She agreed.

The boy was smart and intelligent. He wanted to raise his family from the humble position. He studied very hard. He passed his 10th and 12th exam with distinction. Then came the hardest part.His college education. With the help of his mentor Madhari he could go to a prestigious college and finish his college education. His mother's only ambition was that he should try for I.A.S. Exam. He was trying his best. He failed in his 1st attempt. But he succeeded in the 3rd attempt.

Veena was overwhelmed with emotions. She could not either cry or laugh. She was a plump person. She was worn out with poverty and hard work and unfulfilled wishes. She thought she will collapse on knowing the news somehow she stood erect and blessed her son, tears flowing continuously". "Why are crying mummy", our bad days are over".

This is not tears of sorrow. These are tears of joy. Said Veena half crying and half laughing. He touched her feet and sought her blessings. Her son Pramod was in love with a girl form his IAS batch who also hails from U.P. But she was from an upper class educated family. Pramod told her about his family background!. She said "It does not matter to me. I love you and that is the only important thing to me". Pramod told his mother about the girl. Veena was little apprehensive about the whole thing. But her husband told "Let him decide his own life. Not like us" we were thrown by fate together. But we made it a success. But let him decide whatever he wants".

We can go tour native place and live our old age peacefully. So the matter was settled. The marriage was performed with the blessing of both families.

Both Pramod and Mita were posted in one place, Pramod wanted to bring his parents to stay with them. But Mita objected to the idea. She disliked her uneducated in-laws from the very beginning. So they were sent to U.P. after repairing their old ancestral house. Pramod was sending a fixed amount every month, so they had a comfortable life. Veena's wish to see her son in his new position as a Collector enjoys life, and forget all her hardship and humiliations nevermaterialized.

- o O o -

FLASH FICTION OLD AGE

An old man sat near the entrance of the shop on a stool, but he was not in uniform. His white shirt was a little frayed at the collar and sleeves, and he wore khaki trousers. We both looked at each other simultaneously. There was a flicker of recognition in his eyes, and he was about to speak to me. It was a small shop, and a young man, meticulously dressed, stood at the counter.

It had been five years since I last visited that shop. I had purchased several ceiling fans from there for our new house and farmhouse. I was introduced to the shop owner, Mr. Khilachandani, as an honest and decent gentleman by my friend Mrs. Sindhu Joshi.

Now, he looked old and haggard. At that moment, the young man at the counter greeted me with, "Hello Madam, welcome to the shop," asserting his presence.

I focused on climbing the wooden stairs leading to the shop. As soon as I entered, he greeted me with a polite Namaste and asked how he could assist me. Without further ado, I informed him that I needed a small fan for my bedroom, where an AC was already installed.

The old man cast fleeting glances at me, but I couldn't decipher them. After the formalities, I handed over the cheque. He said, "Madam, it will take another 10-15 minutes for the fan to be brought from the godown." I replied, "I'm in a hurry, so please arrange to send the fan to my residence." "I know you are Mrs. Joshi's friend. I know your address. You have purchased many fans from our shop." "Yes, of course," I said.

His son stepped out to instruct the employee. The old man said, "I am Khilachandani. He is my son. He manages the business now. I have grown old, so he treats me like an employee. I provided him with a good education. I transferred the business into his name. That was the biggest mistake I made. Last year, my wife passed away. Now, he treats me like a servant. He asked me not to come to the shop. But how else am I supposed to spend my time? This is the pathetic condition of many elders in today's society."

- o 0 o -

LIVE IN RELATIONSHIP

Mrs. Mrinal Roy was worried about her only daughter Sara. She wanted to pursue her degree in Master's from a foreign university. Mrunal's husband was working in Atomic Energy in Bombay as a Manager. The salary was not bad. But back home in Calcutta his old parents were there. He had to send a certain amount every month for their maintenance. So Sara's ambition put them in a precarious position. Mr.Biswajeet Roy had to procure a loan on his Provident Fund to pay for her education. Sara got admission in Boston University and settled in U.S.A.

One day Sara called her mother from Boston and said she is very happy. She found a proper guy as her life partner and she was shifting to his apartment and they will move in together as Live in partners. Mrinal was very disturbed. She cautioned her daughter to get full details of her boyfriend's family history, educational qualification and his personal details.

"Mamma are you doing a matrimonial alliance or are you kidding. He is in the teaching faculty. He is doing Ph.D. and we get along very well. His name is S.D. Topiwala and I think he is a Gujarati. That is all I know about him and I think that is enough for you also. I am late for my class. Bye with that she disconnected the phone.

Next time when Mrinal phoned, Sara shifted to her boyfriend's apartment. She seems to be very happy. Mrinal wanted to know more about her partner's details. But Sara is always in a hurry to go to University. She is phoning only in the morning. Why not in the evening? This question was haunting Mrinal. But she kept quiet fearing Sara will not phone her if she becomes more inquisitive. So this continued for 6 or 7 months.

One day Sara phoned Mrinal in the evening. She was crying hysterically. "Sara what happened. Why are you crying ?".Tell me Mrinal asked her.

"Mummy my partner Danish DilkushTopiwala is a Muslim. I think I am pregnant, it is three months. When I raised the question of marriage, he said accordingto Islam, being a Hindu is a Kafir. I have to convert to

Islam if at all I have to marry him. I said "I will never change my religion to get married. So we broke up. I have found an apartment and shifted there with another female student.

"Sara my dear, you come to Bombay immediately. We will find some solution". "This is the end of my final term I will come only after the exam. Mrinal told her husband her daughter's plight. He exploded "You have spoilt her and now you only manage this rotten affair. Now we will not be able to face our people here in Bombay.

"She is coming next month. Bear with her. Otherwise she will break. She is our own daughter, Said Mrinal. Mrinal was crying continuously. "I have a friend Dr. DebMukerji. He is a Gynaec. He will get the abortion done and he will never divulge the facts to anybody. With this assurance of her husband Mrinal retired for the night.

In the meantime, Sara's exam over, she came back to India. She was trying for a job and never wanted to return to America. The parents were circulating the story. She got married and the husband was beating her. So she had to resort to divorce. Sara's friends advised her to file a case against Danish which Sara refused. When it came for the sanction of maternity leave, Sara fearing she had to divulge her marriage details resigned from the job.

Sara saved her five to six months' salary. She delivered a healthy baby girl. After the delivery, Sara stayed at home only for a period of four months. Then she got a good job. The salary was good. She hadto attend office only twice in a week. Saturday and Sunday were holidays. She kept a nanny for the baby so that her child will not be a burden on her mother. But Mrinal adopted her grand-daughter. Her husband Biswajeet initially resisted, but ultimately he could not ignore the baby. Mrinal took full responsibility of the baby. Then came G20. Sara was selected in the team. Sara was intelligent. But she was a failure in the matter of love. She was sending costly clothes, toys to the baby. Every day she will phone and enquire about the baby.

During her one trip to Boston, she met Danish. He was in a mall with his wife, a Muslim girl in Hijab Sara now understood Danish's mentality. She said a feeble hai to him and moved to another section.

Sara's mother was telling her often to find someone. We will not be there forever so you need someone in your old age.We gave our name to your daughter in school. She will be known as our child. Find somebody to suit your temperament. Sara only said "Yes Mama". But she never wanted to marry. When she was on a deputation to America she met a middle aged man, maybe he is 8 to 10 years older than her. He was a Bengali.

"Are you a Bengali". Yes, I am" said Sara. So their friendship grew. In the very first meeting he said I am a Bengali. My name is Anoop Sanyal. I am working in the same section. Hope we meet often. I am single and ready to mingle. "Yes sure" said Sara and moved on. He was very friendly. Sara was trying to withhold her feelings against his charm. One day exasperated he asked her why are you resisting my friendly gestures with your silence.

"Once I am hurt by somebody and still I am nursing the wound in my heart. It will take time the wound to be healed. Give me some time said Sara earnestly.

"Take your own time. I am single and ready to mingle. He said jokingly. Sara blushed and shook his hands. The friendship grew and slowly Sara opened up to him. She told her past which she never wanted to open up to anybody.

Anoop was a widower. He lost his wife during Covid. They had no children and they were very much in love. Sara told him about her daughter whom her parents have adopted. Now I have no legal rights on her. But still I love her.

I also love children said Anoop and then he fell silent. Sara told her mother about Anoop. She was very happy. When Sara said he is little older, she kept quiet. She knows Sara is very adamant and she will do whatever she thinks proper. She will never listen to anybody. She will have her own ways. Mrinal told her daughter. "Marry him if he asks you that are all I can say".

Next week Sara told her mother the good news Anoop unconditionally agreed to marry her and even take care of the baby if Sara wants. He is very fond of children. Mrinal heaved a sigh of relief. When she told her husband the news, he felt relieved and said after all she did a sensible thing, otherwise the girl is impossible and sat on the sofa with relief written all over his face. Mrinal thought my daughter found some happiness ultimately. I must thank God and went towards her Puja room.

- o 0 o -

HEINOUS CRIME

She was frail and tiny. In the quiet corners of Chembur, a suburb in Bombay there lived a family migrated from Ratnagiri. Mother Sundanda father Sunil. One brother and two sisters lived on top of a building in one room. The father was a watchman. So a room was allotted. Sunanda was working as a maid in a nearby colony. Sarala a tiny figure, she carried the weight of her humble beginning. They were a close knit family.

Sarala was keen to pursue her high school education. She was not a bright student. But she was studious. In 8th standard, she got admission in a good school. She failed in the 8th standard and repeated the class. She scrapped through 9th and 10th exam.

With the help of a social worker who came in contact with the family, she got a job in a call centre. A job at call centre brought her a taste of financial freedom. She indulged herself in new clothes, accessories and fancy things. Her family's financial condition as known to her, but she ignored it.

Call centre was at Parel. She had to travel every day. By this time, she gained some weight. Though her feature was not refined, she was fair and became plump and the youthfulness made her attractive. However, the gentle breeze of love began to stir in Sarala's heart with it both enchantment and despair. She met Dilkush who was very stylish and attractive.

He belonged to a different world and faith. A romance ignited yet its flames were tempered by unattainability. Sarala want security but Dilkhush wanted them to enjoy life as it comes.

Sarala was 20 now. She spent most of her earnings on herself. Sunanda was very much hurt.

One day, Sunanda was crying hysterically in the evening. Her husband asked her "What the matter is". Sunanda between her sobs told her husband Sarala had left home and gone to stay with her boyfriend in a "live in relationship". What is that "Live in relationship"! "It is two people living together as husband and wife without marriage". Sunil looked bereft of all senses and his face looked pale. Recovering he said to his wife "Ask her to meet me, I will convince her". These ideas are for affluent people.

When Sunil met Sarala, "what mummy is saying. These ideas are for affluent folks. Not people like us. You help us tide all our financial difficulties for some time. Byethe time, you will better understand your boyfriend. We have two more daughters. I need not tell you this.

"Yes Papa, I will try to help you. With that Sarala went back to Dilkush and their nest. Sometimes, she used to give Sunanda some little money. Sarala thought her boyfriend is a very good person. They used to argue a lot, but he loved her. He used to make breakfast for her. Order food in the night sometimes helps her cleaning the dishes. So it was a cozy life. Some more time passed.

Sunanda put lot of pressure on Sarala. "You and your boyfriend get married soon. I have got more girls to be married".

Sarala on the rebound started putting pressure on Dilkush exasperated Dilkush shouted at her. "I told you repeatedly, we were not in a financial sound position to get married. Wait for some more time. I will get a better jobs and better salary. But Sarala was constantly pressurizing him for the marriage. It was created a lot of friction between them.

One day the argument went for a long time. During one of their fight Dilkush became tense and irritated. He gave her a slap. Sarala got infuriated. My mother or father never beat me, how dare you slap me".

Next day she left the flat and went to her mother's house. Dilkush came and pleaded with her to return. Inspire of her mother's protest Sarala went back with Dilkush. Then started again the arguments and counter arguments.

One day Dilkush asked Sarala to meet his family. His mother, father and one sister and two brothers. His father was a mechanic working in a garage. Sarala felt no connection with them. There was a barrier which she would not decipher. They advised both of them to wait for some more time to get married. If they want to stay with them Sarala had to convert to Islam. Sarala was disheartened. The situation worsened day by day. Sarala was desperate. One day when they were arguing Dilkush said I will kill you, if you behave like this. Sarala got really scared.

Sarala phoned her best friend Tanuja and started crying. Tanuja told her to leave Dilkush immediately and return to her mother's place. Dilkush was listening to her phone talk. He did not get to know what Tanuja advised her.

He did not get to know what Tanuja advised her. For a few days everything was quiet. Sarala thought

Dilkush got intimated by her threat to leave him. But on the contrary, he was planning meticulously to eliminate Sarala who became a liability in his life.

Things looked pretty easy for some more days. It was a Saturday Dilkush ordered pizza and cake and put music and both were dancing. Suddenly Sarala asked him "when will we get married".

"Never" Dilkush said with so much emphasis on the word "Never". Sarala got a shock.

"Then we should not stay together. I am leaving for my mother place and never return". We were in good mood. Why you started your parrot like phrase "when are we getting married", it irritates me you know. So you have become a spoilt sport. We cannot continue like this anymore". What do you mean by anyone "Sarala retorted angrily. I mean what I said "said Dilkush in an angry tone". Don't use that tone again". You are threatening me. Dilkush was angry. There was a hammer lying on the side table which he used for fixing a photo frame. He took it and hit her at the back of her head. Instantly, she collapsed on the floor, with a thud. Dilkush went to support her. She screamed. Don't touch me. You are a mean person. You used me and now discarding me like a rotten apple. Then she became unconscious. After sometime her breathing become heavier and suddenly it stopped. Blood was oozing out of her head. He tried to make her sit. But she was dead. Dilkush got really scared. His first reaction was to call the doctor. Then he saw there was no breathing that means she is dead. He coolly went to the door and locked it. Then he meticulously cleaned the whole area and put her body under the cot. Earlier he drank some bear. Now he opened a bottle of whisky and drank and went and slept on the cot. He got up at about 5 O' clock and realised the seriousness of the whole situation. He went to a nearby Mall and purchased a sharp knife to cut her body into pieces. He also purchased a suit case big enough to put all the parts to dispose of. He was waiting for night, where it was dark enough he went with the suitcase.

The watchman was curious. But he was scared to ask him. So he went out without any remorse.

Next few days the same pattern continued. But Dilkush took care to go out when the watchman was not there. Next day after two days of the murder. Tanuja phoned. She was curious for her friend's safety. Dilkush said Sarala went to her mother's house two days back. Tanuja phoned Sunanda. Sunanda said Sarala had not came to their house. Tanuja phoned the police. Police started searching for Sarala. When they could not get any whereabouts of Sarala, they called Dilkush for enquiry. What scene unfolded before the police was all a pack of lies. Police arrested Dilkush.

Ultimately Dilkush was found guilty of the murder and sentenced to life imprisonment.

Here Sunanda took rat poison and got saved in nick of time. So it was a sensational news item. But for Sunanda's family, it was a disaster. Her husband had a paralytic stroke. Emotionally and financially they were drained because the silliness of a daughter. Sarala was smart. She could have sensed Dilkush intentions. But she was in love with him. Love is blind. So many untoward things happen which could have easily avoided, if you are cautious.

- o 0 o -

L.G.B.T.Q. NEWS

It was the British Era. Our village was selected among 15 small villages to have a primary school and a public well. The main reason for the selection of the village was once, it was a small princely Kingdom called Vasupura, then became Basupura. The hill on which the school building was to be constructed, was the place where the King's palace once stood. The big wall surrounding the hill on all sides, was there in dilapidated condition. The palace was surrounded by deep trenches of 25 feet on both sides of the fort. During an enemy attack, the trenches were filled with water. It is still there and in monsoon fills with water.

During the digging of the place, many artifacts were found. Once during the digging of the place a metal box containing gold and silver coins with a idol of Lord Shiva in silver was found, which was immediately confiscated and handed over to the Dy.Collector a English man with all the pomp and show by the village Pramukh.

All the villagers rejoiced the event, our houses and main entrances of the village was decorated with Marigold flowers and Mango leaves. The construction was nearing completion. The Bhumi Pujan was done by the Dy. Collector and the school building started functioning. Then a new problem surfaced.

The school building was functioning in two shifts from 9.00 to 2.30 and 2.00 to 5.00 P.M. Climbing the hill twice a day, was it felt for the small chest burn. So a new structure was constructed in the middle of the village for the primary students.

Lata's house was very near to the primary school. The admission starts after completion of six years. Lata's mother used to admit her childern after completion of 4 years. The teacher used to ask the usual question. What is the age? What is the date of birth? Lata"s mother was ready with the answer. Just completed 6 years and date of birth is so and so which she kept ready. Some of her burden would be shared by the school. So we all started schooling at the age of 4 instead of 6.

Chandrika and Lata were best friend. Her father was a marginal farmer and he was helping the village

Patil in his work to augment his income. After two girls Saket was born. It was found he was not a girl nor a boy. He was a transgender. His mother was heartbroken. But after two girls they decided to bring him up as a boy. In the month of June, Chandrika's father got a fever.

After the 1st showers in June, it was a normal thing. He took some medicine and the fever went on increasing, instead of abating. It was pneumonia, he died on the 6th day with unabating fever and lung infection. Chandrika's mother was devastated. But she could not relax.

The burden of three children and the house fell in her. She also started assisting the village Pramukh in his work. She started working in two houses for an hour orso as a cook. Somehow she was managing.

Chandrika and Lata were best friends from 1st standard. They were in the 3rd standard when her kid brother started attending school. There were two toilets one for the boys and one for girls. The boys out numbered the girls. There was a vast surrounding open area where the boys used to go for 1st call. But Chandrika's brother never used to go in the open area. Chandrika always accompanied him to the toilet. There was another girl by the name called Rajani, who was our common friend. Rajani was a curious cat. She used to follow Saket to the toilet. This irritated Chandrika.

They both fought on this issue. They were not on talking terms.

They all passed 3rd standard and started going to the Hill school. Unfortunately Rajani failed in the 3rd standard. Now Chandrika was not there to protect Saket. One day Rajani sneaked into the toilet when Saket was there and a rumour was circulated that Saket was neither a boy or a girl. A transgender.Rajani's one brother was a practicing Lawyer in Madras High Court. She learnt the word from him.

Village people were not knowing who is a transgender. Some people with growth of hair on their faces wearing sarees came for alms on Saturday the alms day in the village. They were called Chakkas.

Unlike in the northern states, these people were never called on any auspicious occasion like child birth or marriage in our villages. In the northern states, they are invited on such occasion to bless baby or the couple.

Chandrika before completion of her secondary education got married. She came to give Lata her marriage card. They both got emotional. They both hugged each other and cried. Lata attended her marriage. Her husband was a nice fellow. Chandrika moved to her husband's place in a nearby village. For some time, both lost touch with each other.

Lata wanted to study further and went to a highs school. Lata and her two friends started going to a high school, after much persuasion The parents agreed for their higher studies. They have to walk about 3 km from the village walking a distance of 6 KM and crossing a river twice and come back in the evening. They were prepared to take any risk and hardship to continue their education. Somehow all three completed their high school.

After the 11th, that is matriculation in those days, Lata got a job in a Government office. she used to go to her village once in a month. She completely lost touch with Chandrika. Once both the friends met in their temple on a festival day. They were busy exchanging news about each other. Chandrika was happy. That is all mattered to her friend. A few more years passed, mother used to write to Lata regularly.

In one letter she wrote that Chandrika came to their house to give wedding card of her brother Saket.

After 20 years, he got hair on his face and he was roaming with a small beard and moustache. He completed his secondary education from our school went to a high school, did a teacher's training course and was teaching in our school. He got a girl from a poor family and married her. Then I got news, he had undergone an operation to become a man. It was a hush hush affairs done in Madras.

In those days, we did not know who is a transgender. Now everything is available in Google and Facebook. Now a new word L.G.B.T.Q. is in circulation and a court battle is won by these people for their rights. Now everybody knows what is L.G.B.T.Q.I.R. L for Lesbians, a girl's orientation towards girls. G for gay, a boys attraction for boys, and B for both sex and T is for transgender. Q is queer. So the world has gone for ahead of those times when everything was a secret and talked in hushed tones.

- o 0 o -

MARRIAGES ARE MADE IN HEAVEN

Janaki was working as a teacher in a primary school. She fell in love with the trustee of the school, a handsome young man without ascertaining his background. He was already a married man, nephew of the original trustee, a poor relative Janaki married him against the wishes of her family. So the family made it very clear to her, that in case she marries him she has to severe all connections with them. Her husband Sridhar had no income of his own.

Sita and Gita, Janaki's daughters were brought up in near poverty. Sita completed her 8th standard and wanted to study further, but there was no high school in their village.

But destiny had other plans. April & May are intensely hot months in India except the hilly parts. Still the villages retain some coolness because of the greenery and sparse population.

Sita's one affluent aunt, came visiting them in 2nd half of May, for a week. During her stay, she saw and sympathized with Janaki. She decided to sponsor Sita's and her sister's stay in her house during their high school education.

Sita moved in with her aunt in June. She got scholarship and started attending school in June in town. She was only 14 when she joined school in the 9th standard.

She was thin, short possessing a weak voice. She exerted effort to make her voice heard. So sometimes it sounded shrill. She was a mischievous child, a teacher in her primary school nicknamed her "Kagemari" in Kannada (crow chic) just to punish her and the nickname struck with. Madhava another student from her village also joined the school. He was staying in his maternal uncle's house whose cousin Sudha also joined them there in the 9th standard. He told Sudha about Sita's nick name.

On the very first day of the school, the girls started ragging Sita "Kagemari" which deeply hurt her. She ran and sat in one corner of the school building crying inconsolably. Sudha and her friend Ramola felt bad and came to pacify Sita. The other girl Ramola, daughter of the science teacher was a kind hearted person, felt sympathetic, felt like crying; hugged Sita while consoling. Soon they become best friends.

Sita'sparents marriage was not recognized by the village hierarchy. Her parents were married in a temple, with no witness only a priest who performed the ceremony. It was like a live in relationship. Sita's father had no income of his own and her life journey was filled with negative comments, disappointments and disapprovals.

Sita's aunt's place was only a few meters away from Ramola's house. Sita started visiting Ramola often. During the three years in High School. Sita underwent a gradual yet tremendous change gaining height and weight evolving into a stunning young women.

The change was gradual, but tremendous. After her Matriculation, Sita secured a job in a Government office.

Ramola often used to invite Sita to her house. They used to study together and at other times, they used to spend their time in Ramola'swell-developed garden.

It was the month of Sravan. An auspicious month for the Hindus. Sita and Ramola were seated on the swing in the garden. They heard the rustling of dry leaves Sita saw Viraj, Ramola's brother advancing towards the swing.

Sita turned to look at the most bewitching eyes of Viraj, Ramola's brother. He was of medium height wore a light pink sleeveless T Shirt and a blue jeans. When their eyes met there was a growling like sound came from Viraj. Ramola saw Viraj and she pulled Sita and they ran towards the main house.Viraj returned to his cottage. He is so handsome thought Sita.

Ramola's father purchased a jersey cow and an indigenously developed mulching machine to their house. Ramola invited Sita to see the process. Sita saw the process and they were fully engrossed looking the process amid the engrossing process, Viraj slowly was coming towards them. There was a soft smile hovering on his lips and a twinkle in his eyes. Viraj and Ramola's eyes met for a second, and then he retreated to his cottage.

Next time Ramola and Sita were seated on the swing. Suddenly it started drizzling Viraj came and sat next to Ramola on the swing. The rain drops glistering on the glass pane of the window of the main house and the rain drops on the lotus leaves looking like pearls were fascinating to see. The many splendors of nature mesmerized Sita. As soon as the rain stopped Viraj left for his cottage. Sita and Romila returned to the main house.

Next time when Sita went to Ramola's house, Viraj was doing some carpentry work in the Veranda of his cottage and on another time he was standing under the Gulmohar tree in full bloom, unaware of everything, Sita returned little disappointed.

Then one day Viraj came and sat on the swing where Ramola and Sita were seated. He asked Ramola "who is this girl. Is she your friend. "What is her name". Viraj addressed Ramola in a soft tone. Those were the first few words he spoke after returning from Banaras.

"Ramola was so excited still she controlled her feeling and said "Sorry bhayya, she is my classmate and friend Sita. I should have introduced her to you. "If you wish she will be your friend also". "Sita nice name "Ram ka Sita" saying this he felt for his cottage.

Ramola pulling Sita ran towards the house to tell her parents about the good news.

At that very moment, the main gate opened and Ramola's father came on his bicycle and he saw Viraj going towards his cottage, he put a gentle hand on his son's shoulder and they both went towards the cottage.

After settling Viraj, his father came to the main house when he heard the news, both he and his wife were happy and were very excited. Now there was a ray of hope.

Ramola and Sita's friendship grew with each passing day. One day Ramola invited Sita to see her rose garden which was in full bloom. Slowly Sita also developed an interest in gardening. The sweat smell of rose wafting through the breeze made them intoxicated by its fragrance. Sita and Ramola simultaneously saw Viraj approaching the swing. Ramola discreetly left on the pretext of helping her mother. Viraj came and sat next to Sita. Sita was only 18 at that time. Viraj found during the talk that Sita was a knowledgeable girl. She had interest in literature, music, gardening, including household work. Viraj was an extrovert. Their friendship grew and slowly they both realized that they were in love.

One day Sita asked Ramola "why is your brother, kept in the outhouse. What is wrong with him? Ramola replied in a voice full of sadness "My brother is very brilliant boy. My father had lots of hopes on him.

He was sent to Banaras Hindu University to study M.Sc. in Agriculture.

He had an aborted love affair. My father had to go to Banaras to bring him back. Since then, he is in this state, sometimes he becomes violent. That is why he had been kept in the outhouse. Tears welled up in her eyes and started flowing. Her father had exhausted each and every avenue in medical science to cure him. Now he had learnt that there is a new doctor who is an expert in treating mentally disturbed patients, in Manipal Hospital. My father had taken an appointment for Baiyya next week.

Next week Mr. Ramnarayan his wife and Viraj sat in their car to go to Manipal. Ramola and Sita were standing near the gate. Suddenly Viraj got down from the car came to Sita and said slowly "I love you". Sita was stunned. She could not utter any words. The car moved on.

Sita knew by instinct Viraj was in love with her. She was madly in love with him. But she never expressed her feelings. There was a question mark in between. Are Viraj's parents ready to accept her, a poor girl with not so a respectful background as daughter-in-law.

The doctor at Manipal Hospital after listening to the recent development thought of changing the line of treatment. An MRI was done to study the condition of the brain. They stayed in Manipal for about a week. He was recovering slowly. After one week, they came back from Manipal both Ramola and Sita decorated the house with marigold flowers and Mango leaves like we do during Deepavali festival. Previous whole week Sita stayed with Ramola.

Viraj came smiling and he was taken to the main house. How is your friend Sita Viraj asked Ramola. Why can't you ask her. She is your friend also.

Now it was routine for Sita to go to Ramola's place every day after work. Doctor advised Viraj complete rest. Sita used to read for Viraj and at other times. Sita found herself captivated by Virajas engaging conversion. Their friendship slowly evolving into love.

Ramola once gave a hint that her one uncle, a noted Kannada author married a non-Brahmin girl and his father was the first one in the family to accept them and welcomed them into the family fold. But here Sita's background is a disadvantage.

Earlier whenever Viraj came to the Swing Ramola silently slipped and left them alone. One day Ramola's mother Jaya admonished Ramola "Ramola are you encouraging their love affairs. I don't like that girl".

Mummy what is your problem. She is a nice girl.

"Because she is your friend, Retorted Jaya". "No because she is basically a nice decent and beautiful girl".

"What about her background". "Her background is her fast. Her future is with us".

"I will not allow this marriage to take place". What our people will say, they will boycott us".

"What happened when Kaka married a non-Brahmin girl, for sometimes they sulked. Now everyone is coming to our place to have lunch on Saturday, the market day with that she returned to her room.

When they retired for the night Ramola's mother told her husband in no uncertain terms her objection for the alliance. Her husband tried to convince her 'see Jaya Viraj suffered a lot and this girl brought some peace and happiness in Viraj's life. He is happy with her. That is all matters to us. Can you find any fault in Sita's behavior except her background? But Iwill not go against your wishes. Think aboutViraj and of the situation and decide, with that the topic was closed.

Eventually, Ramola's mother, Jaya, who initially opposed the marriage, had a change of heart after witnessing Viraj's improvement and their love.

One fine day Ramnarayan called Sita and put the marriage proposal to her, before that he talked to Viraj to ascertain his opinion. When the marriage proposal was put to her Sita was so overwhelmed with emotions, she felt her head was spinning under a flurry of emotions. Tears obscured her vision. She could not hold back her tears. She just touched the feet of her adored teacher and would be father-in-law. He blessedher and the marriage was fixed.

They all knew Sita was a beautiful and principled person. She will be an asset to any family Ramola was very happy for her best friend.

Some of their relatives objected to the marriage because of Sita's background. But Mr. Ramnarayan just ignored them.

Sita's parents came along with her aunt and sister. After doing Kanyadan they returned to their village the same evening. All the expenses were borne by Viraj's father.

Now Viraj was leading a normal life. After recovering from his mental trauma. He started looking after his father's farm and immersed himself in the agriculture research his father had initiated. Sita after resigning from her job, started helping Viraj in the financial aspect of the business. Viraj was a loving husband.

On one Saturday, they all started for their farm about 50 KM from their house for a week and stay. The farm was nestled among hills, one side of it enclosed bya mountain slope and other side by a flowing river where they have made steps to reach the river. When they nearly reached the farm, it started raining. There were many springs on the mountain slope.

As soon as the rain started suddenly the springs came to life and started flowing like magic. The clouds were descending as if from the sky. It was such an enchanting scene. Everyone got mesmerized.

Sita was day dreaming. "What a beautiful scenery! We should visit our farm more often especially in monsoon". Viraj's words suddenly woke up her from her day dream.

"Yes sure" Sita uttered the irrelevant words "What sure Sita" are you day dreaming". Viraj asked. She felt embarrassed. Viraj was driving and he just squeezed her hand. Sita blushed and smiled at him.

Viraj could sense the coy shyness of a newly married girl and simply smiled back at her.

Sita's dream of gaining respect and financially a secure life became a reality. So their poignant love story became a reality. Both were happy.

- o 0 o -

MONKHOOD

Shaku looked at her son for the 1st time after he embraced Monkhood. He was a good looking boy. He was sitting on a chair opposite the news Editor and a bursting crowd. She wanted to embrace him. She thought he was looking resplendent in his orange Monk's attire. She restrained herself by the spectacle before her, a vivid reminder of the turn of events and the intricacies of fate.

It was long time back. The whole scenario flashed across the canvas of her mind. She was a young bride newly married and entered her in-law's house. Her husband was a Govt. employee and he was the only son of his parents. So he told her when he first met her she should not harbor any idea of living separately from his parents so she resigned herself to the idea of living in a joint family. But her in-laws were quite decent people.

She moulded herself to the role of a obedient daughter-in-law. A few years passed peacefully. Shaku did not conceive for a long time. Her mother-in-law started grumbling. Then started the direct accusations. "She is a banj". This hurt Shaku very much. Raghu her husband escaped the jabs. Her name was Shakuntala. Everyone called her "Shaku".

Shaku had to undergo IVF treatments 3 times. Finally the 3rd time she conceived. Her mother-in-law made her comfortable as far she could do. She was advised bed rest. So she was sent to her mother's place for rest. Here the scene has changed after her brother's marriage. Her mother was a meek person and her bhabhi was managing the whole house.

Shaku had to bear the brunt of her bhabhi's barbs and taunts. Somehow nine months passed without any major incidents.

In the end, she had to undergo a caesarian delivery and a healthy boy was born. Shaku looked at her son and all her hardships disappeared in a moment. After two months, she came to her husband's place. It was a joyous occasion. The whole house was decorated. A pooja was kept. All their dear and near relatives were invited. A beaming Shaku stood near the cradle and greeted each and every guest. Her mother-in-law was running from bedroom to kitchen as if she is on wing. Such a happy atmosphere was there. The boy was named Vivek after the great saint Swami Vivekananda.

Six months maternity leave got exhausted. Shaku had to join duty in her school. It was the month of March. 1½ months was left for the summer holidays. Somehow reluctantly she joined duty as a teacher. Each day was a trial by fire for Shaku to leave her son at home and go to work. Time was flying. Vivek started going to the nursery. Shaku and Vivek started going together and come back together.

Raghu also taking a keen interest in his son's studies. So Vivek stood always first in his class. His teachers were amazed at his memory which is called photographic memory. Vivek passed his 12th exam with distinction. Both Shaku and Raghu were very happy.

Then he had to decide which course he will opt. He had already decided for engineering in IIT in Bombay. From Bihar to Bombay, a great journey. Vivek's father was in a clerical post. His son's desire was ultimate in their house. So Raghu took a loan from his Provident Fund and Vivek's B.Tech was completed. Vivek decided to further study for his M.Tech in V.J.T.I. in Bombay.

The financial aspect was never his concern. He told his parents he will complete his M.Tech and then he will get a job with fat salary. Mr. Raghu suggested Vivek to take an education loan from a bank. But Shaku intervened. "Why trouble him with financial aspects, when he is studying. No bank loan. "We can mortgage our house. Vivek can easily pay back the loan. So two years passed without any hitch.

When Vivek was in Bombay one of his friends introduced him to Guruji in Hare Krishna temple in Juhu. Vivek started going regularly to the Ashram at the fag end of his final year. Vivek was basically a chilled out person. He was intelligent and study was never a problem. Now when he thought of the rat race in the job market he was little scared. He was a religious person for that matter, his whole family was religious. So slowly he decided to become a monk. The atmosphere in Hare Krishna was so tension free his decision to join Ashram strengthened his thoughts, yet fate took an unexpected turn with his decision to embrace monkhood leaving his parents to grappling with a sense of loss and bewilderment

When they came to know a press conference was held and his son was also there. Shaku and Raghu decided to attend the conference. Shaku was continuously staring at her son. Once or twice their eyes met and he immediately averted his gaze and looked in another direction.

After the press conference, Shaku and Raghu met him for a brief period. Shaku cried like a small child. "Don't leave us and go I cannot live without you. You can still reverse your decision. But he was not listening to her. He had decided his path. He went back with his group.

Shaku's husband actually dragged her from the avenue. Shaku was hysterical. Mr. Raghu also got exhausted. Then both sat in their car and Raghu started his car towards their homeward journey with a blank expression on his face.

He was unable to apprehend what made his son join monkhood. In another two years, he will retire and the pension he gets is barely sufficient for their living. But the loan on the house is a big burden. The whole Provident Fund money will not be sufficient to clear the loan on the house. The dreams of travel and leisure eclipsed by the harsh realities of life.

As time marched on Shaku gripped with feelings of inadequacy and regret, questioning Her role as a mother and her inability to alter the course of her son's destiny. So in the end she decided to join her duty as a teacher to transgress the loneliness and emptiness. She found glimmers of hope buoyed by the unwavering support by her husband and the passage of time.

In the end they emerged from their trails and their heart scarred but unscratched. For Shaku the journey had been one of profound self-discovery a testament to the resilience of the human spirit though their path have been fraught with challenges and heart breaks. They found solace in the knowledge that they had faced the trials together hand in hand forging a bond that would withstand the test of time.

- o 0 o -

SHANTA

Shanta vividly remembered that faithful day some 13 years ago. Thirteen years is a long period. Each and every details of that day etched like a colourful picture in the canvas of her memory.

Shanta was excited. They hardly hard any guests in recent times. On a Saturday early morning, a chaffier driver Ambassador car stood opposite their house in the narrow lane. Neighbours peeped out of their houses to see the guests. Shanta was most excited. They prepared a sumptuous breakfast of idli, vada, sambhar and chutney, some banana chips and filter coffee. The old filter was removed from the attic cleaned and coffee was ready.

After the breakfast the guests asked Anant Kamath, Shanta's father, his permission to take Shanta alongwith them to the Mukambika Temple at Kollur. They were on their way to visit the temple of Mukambika at Kollur.

AnantKamath was a teacher in a secondary school in Koni, a village near Kundapur. He had an ancestral house with a small patch of paddy field along with some coconut trees. He was a good teacher but very strict. So none of the children liked him.

He had three daughters. Sumitra 14, Shanta 12 and Praful 10. His wife breathed her last during the delivery of her son. He was named Shantanu. Mr. Anant Kamat not used to the responsibilities of the house, married again. None of his daughters were happy. His second wife Laxmi came from a poor family, she was above the marriageable age by Indian standards. But she was a kind hearted person.

Sumitra his eldest daughter after completing her 7th standard did a course in stitching and tailoring and started earning some money. The 2nd daughter Shanta was Anant's favourite. He always wished her the best. Shanta was cool, intelligent and beautiful. He knew Shanta wanted to study further.

Those were the days everybody was poor in the village. There were no tuitions in those days.

So it was beyond his means.

The guests who came, were Laxmi's cousin sister, her husband and their children. Laxmi's cousin Mohini was married to a banker. In the course of time, he rose to the position of a manager. He was a manager in Syndicate Bank, Udipi Branch. He had two daughters and a son.

After returning from the temple, Mr. Shankar, Mohini, Anant and Laxmi had a close room meeting. Mohini and her husband convinced Anant that they wanted to take Shanta alongwith them to Udipi. She will be admitted to a school there and Shanta will help Mohini in the house. Ananta wanted the best for Shanta, so he agreed to their proposal. No financial aspect was discussed. Shanta was packed off to Udipi without her consent.

Earlier Shanta thought it is impossible for her to study further. She decided to do a teacher's training course and work as a teacher like her father. But the above decision of her parents jostled her out of her dreams. She hated her father and step mother. She thought her step mother was responsible for her present state. But she also knew her father, nobody can influence him. She thought she had been sent as a maid to Udipi. She had no choice. She went along with Mohini and her family to Udipi. She was crying silently. After a month or so, she came to know a certain fixed amount was sent to her father every month. Her doubt was confirmed. Realizing this her heart broke.

Shanta used to get up early, finish cooking breakfast, lunch, attend the school in the afternoon and study in the night. Mohini's one daughter Priya also was studying for medicine. Shanta used to study along with her. Shanta completed her 12th exam and passed with distinction. Mohini celebrated the event throwing a grand party.

The entire Shenoi family treated her like a family member. They took her on holidays along with them. In spite of all their efforts to make her happy, she was unhappy with her father.

At this juncture, Mr. Shenoy was transferred to Bombay. They were all very happy specially Priya who liked the anonymity of big city.

Priya, Mohini's daughter completed her M.B.B.S. after undergoing training and internship period of 1 ½ years in a rural area. She passed the M.B.B.S. exam in 1st class. There was a celebration in Shenoy's house. Then came a rude shock. Priya was in love with a merchant navy captain a handsome Punjabi boy, whom she wanted to marry.

Priya never confided in her mother. Only Shanta had some inkling of it, but she was tight lipped. When the news reached Mohini more than anything else Mohini's ego was hurt. She was a very dominating person. Whatever she decides was carried out without any opposition. When they were newly married Shanker her husband tried to put some sense in Mohini, not to have her own way. He was a peace loving person. For the domestic peace and harmony he let Mohini have her own way.

Mohini opposed the marriage on the ground the boy was not of their caste. He was a Punjabi. Priya and her beau Vicky got married in a Civil court. Priya was thrown out of the house. She stayed in the college hostel for 2 years and finished her post-graduation in general medicine. After that they rented a house in Worli and started living there.

Otherwise the quite house of Shenoi's was completely disturbed. After the storm some peace prevailed. In that turbulent period Mohini's one nephew, her sister's son Raghu was transferred to Mumbai. He was working in Canara Bank and stayed in the Bachelor quarters. On weekends he used to visit Mohini.

There was a vacancy in his bank and Raghu requested Mohini to let Shanta apply for the job. Shanta got the job and Shanta even after getting the job, was doing her duty as usual. She used to get up early, finish all her work, pack her Tiffin and go to Bank. It was a back breaking job. But Shanta was always efficient andsmiling.

A few more years passed. Mohini's daughter got married and the son after completing his Electrical

Engineering married a girl working in a pharmaceutical company. Mohini made her leave the job and stay at home to help her. Raghu was waiting for an opportunity. He confided in Mohini his liking for Shanta and his wish to marry her. Mohini was also worried about Shanta's future. She immediately agreed. She wanted to have a grand marriage. But Shanta opposed the idea. She said a simple court marriage and a party at home for a few people was all. Mohini wanted to send an invitation to Mr. Anant. Shanta opposed it. In reply only a telegram blessing the couple came.

Shanta and her husband shifted to their own house in Chembur. Both were working in Banks and loan was easily available to them. Even after settling up her house, Shanta used to go and help Mohini wherever she was in need.

Shanta's husband Raghu told her many times to go and meet her father. But Shanta was unable to forget or forgive. She was pestering a wound in her heart which was like poison and her heart was still bleeding.

Then one day she got news that her father was dying. He was repeatedly asking for Shanta. Raghu forced Shanta to go and meet her father in his dying time. Reluctantly Shanta went to meet him.

On seeing his condition, all her hatred melted and she just touched his feet in obedience. For a moment her heart stopped beating. She was crying uncontrollably. He breathed his last holding her hands and asking her forgiveness for whatever wrong he did. All her pent up feelings like anger, hatred vanished.

She returned with love and peace, the old Shanta, poignant memories of good old days with her father flooded her memory. She realised each and every one had in innate desire to be heard and she denied this right to her father, a mistake she did unknowingly.

- o 0 o -

MUSIC TEACHER

Gauri, a young woman of striking beauty and unwavering determination, harbored dreams of becoming a teacher. She had finished her secondary education. However, the absence of a nearby high school thwarted her aspirations for further education. Theirs was a modern family. Her father had retired by then, and her brother had become the village Pramukh, a post that her father held before retiring. The brother was a modern young individual with great aspirations. He had started renovating their old house to have a better household space for the family. It was one of his goals to have a beautiful home where his family could spend all their time together.

Their endeavor brought Sakharam, a diploma holder from Mangalore, into their midst. Sakharam, the young man from Mangalore, was tall, fair, and had an impressive personality. Given his charming personality, he was popular with the younger generation, especially the ladies.

Gauri, having reached a marriageable age, started receiving proposals for marriage. Gauri and her family belonged to the Brahmin community. Most of the grooms from the Brahmin community would wear a tuft, showcasing their orthodox upbringing. Gauri detested that trait.

A couple of guys among the prospects were without the tuft but were not particularly good-looking. It was proving to be quite difficult to find her a good match for marriage as Gauri did not like any of the suitors. On the other hand, during the search for a groom for Gauri, Sakharam's presence captivated Gauri's eye amidst the flurry of marriage proposals she received. Despite social barriers, Gauri found herself drawn to Sakharam, realizing that traditional Brahmin suitors did not match with her views.

As their bond grew, Gauri's mother, perturbedby their growing closeness, urged her husband to intervene. One day she told her husband, "Remove that Sakharam from the job, or we will have a huge crisis in our family." The father did not ascribe too much importance to the mother's fears and took the situation rather lightly. He quipped, "My Gauri opting for a Gowda boy, impossible!"

Every Saturday evening, Gauri would visit the Hanuman temple. This one time, Gauri did not return from the temple till late. She would usually be back home by 8 pm on Saturdays. The parents sent her brother to look for her as it started to get pretty late. He came back home after looking for her in 15 minutes in a very agitated mood. The Pujari at the temple had told him that he had seen Gauri and Ram going from the temple together dressed in fine clothes towards the bus depot. From the village, there was a bus that would leave for Bombay at 8 pm on Saturdays. Her father, who usually was a very relaxed man, yelled, "Somebody go right now to the bus station and enquire." The brother rushed to the bus station,but by the time he reached the station, the bus to Bombay had left.

He came back running to the house to break the news. The family decided to go to the police station to lodge a missing report. The cops at the station were helpful, but they told them that they could not take a missing persons report until 24 hours had elapsed. The family members were in extreme distress the entire night. They were sure Gauri had eloped with Ram. They still had left the doors half-open, hoping Gauri would come back.

Gauri and Ram arrived in Mumbai the following morning, where Ram's sister resided. The sister was working in Bombay as a nurse and was staying in a chawl with one of her friends, where she had a small space. For their initial night, Ram secured lodging at a modest hotel, intending to relocate to the sister's residence the following day. They planned to go back to the house in the morning. However, assessing the conditions prevailing in Mumbai, Gauri found herself contemplating a return to her hometown, bracing for the anticipated disapproval from her family.

Upon their return to Bangalore, Gauri realized that Ram's house in Bangalore was not well kept. Ram and his family were non-vegetarians. Their house had a distinct smell of fish, which is common in fish-eating households. Gauri, being a vegetarian, found the smell nauseating. The house was not clean either Displeased with the overall cleanliness standards, she promptly compiled a list of essential supplies, including room fresheners, hand wash, napkins, and soap, to attend the hygiene deficiencies she observed. She started cleaning the house herself; it seemed like a Herculean task. Her mother-in-law tried to help her, but she was not adept at the task at hand. Gauri valiantly tackled the task, and by afternoon, the house was spick and span.

In an unexpected turn of events at 2 o'clock, law enforcement officials arrived at Ram's doorstep, prompting Gauri to personally engage with them. Gauri told the cops that she was over 18 years old and that she was free to make her own decisions regarding her marriage. She told the cops, "I have married Ram with my own will, and I very well know the consequences of deciding to marry him." Her articulate and composed response not only surprised the police but also conveyed a profound sense of conviction behind her decision. The police conveyed Gauri's decision to her family and relayed her reasoning to them. The family, after hearing the news, relinquished any lingering hopes of her return.

Gauri and Ram resided in Bombay for two days before returning to Bangalore. Despite their return, Ram encountered difficulty securing meaningful employment locally due to a lack of support from the community. Ram possessed a remarkable talent for deciphering various handwriting styles and demonstrated proficiency in penmanship. Recognizing his potential, Gauri encouraged him to refine his skills, eventually suggesting he explore the art of calligraphy. Taking this suggestion, Ram embarked on his calligraphy journey, subsequently transitioning to drafting legal documents for court proceedings. Through his new role, he came in contact with a lot of lawyers. Consequently, when villagers faced challenges, they sought recourse and guidance at Ram's residence, elevating his stature as a respected figure within the community and earn a lot of money.

Several years following their marriage, Gauri's father passed away, leaving her brother Aditya to manage the family affairs. Despite the opposition, Aditya welcomed Gauri back into the familial fold, yet Ram remained estranged from full acceptance into the family.

Over time, Gauri and Ram expanded their family, Gauri was blessed with six sons and two daughters. Their eldest son, Anand, distinguished himself with his striking appearance and innate musical talent. Possessing a keen interest in music, Anand pursued formal studies up to the 8th grade before dedicating himself to Karnataka music, studying under the tutelage of Guru Laxman Acharya. Regrettably, his mentor's premature demise halted his musical education prematurely. Anand, driven by ambition, sought opportunities in larger cities like Bombay or Bangalore. To support himself, at the age of 18, he commenced imparting music lessons to the village youth. Among his students was Veena, the daughter of Gauri's brother, known for her loving nature. Anand, nurturing a fondness for her, provided her with special attention and guidance in her musical endeavors. The two went on to have a very strong student and teacher bond. Veena respected Anand for his musical acumen and also admired her uncle's discipline and love for the craft of music.

Anand and Gauri's house help had a daughter named Meena. She was married to her maternal uncle, Krishna. Krishna was an old man while Meena was young. Despite the significant age gap between them, societal pressures compelled Meena into this union. Before her marriage, Meena maintained a close friendship with Salim, who harbored romantic feelings for her. Even after her marriage to Krishna, Salim continued to visit her under the guise of learning the art of weaving from Krishna. One day Meena and Salim eloped and ran away to Bombay to live together. Salim had no educational qualification nor was he trained in any occupation. The two of them found it difficult to make ends meet in Bombay. With limited education and vocational skills, they found themselves compelled to engage in work at a brothel to sustain themselves in the metropolis. They started earning good money, and Meena would carry a lot of gifts back to the village every time she visited home. Encouraged by Meena and Salim's apparent success and unsure of their own source of income, Anand ventured to Bombay to pursue his passion for music. During his visit to Bombay, Anand reunited with Meena and Salim, who painted a picture of the city as a land of boundless opportunities. Inspired by their encouragement, Anand eagerly embarked on this new chapter of his life, wholeheartedly dedicating himself to pursuing his musical aspirations. However, despite his earnest efforts, he encountered a stark reality. He tried with all dedication to find opportunities, but no one in Mumbai was interested in learning Karnataka music. For a brief period, Anand resided with Meena and Salim, hoping for a breakthrough. Yet, faced with the harsh economic realities of the city, he eventually found himself relegated to the streets, where he endured the hardships of homelessness, forced to sleep on footpaths due to financial constraints preventing him from securing accommodation.

One day while he was struggling to sleep on the footpath, plagued with extreme hunger, a henchman of Bombay's city's top mafia boss found him. Through earnest conversation, Anand shared his plight and background with the henchman. The henchman found him to be an honest and forthright person. He promised him a job in the city. The henchman gave Anand the job of collecting Hafta from the roadside vendors. Anand exhibited exemplary integrity and meticulousness in his duties, consistently delivering all collections to his superior with unwavering honesty. His diligent work ethic and steadfast commitment garnered recognition, enabling him to swiftly rise among the ranks. During his visits to the village, he shared his success by sending both funds and gifts. Everyone in the village was happy given his success in the city, but no one knew of the nature of Anand's work in the city. Despite his newfound prosperity, Anand maintained secrecy regarding the nature of his employment, concealing it from both his village and his own family.

Back in his village, Veena Gauri's brother Aditya's daughter had completed in her education by now, completing high school. Her parents, seeking a suitable match for her, arranged a marriage with a prosperous engineer within their community. As plans were made for the wedding, Veena desired her uncle Anand's presence and extended an invitation to him. However, Anand, engrossed in his commitments in Bombay, expressed difficulty in taking leave to attend the ceremony. Despite his reservations, fate intervened. Amidst the summer season, a period when many from Bombay frequented Konkan for summer vacation, Anand, in his elevated position, remained tied to his responsibilities. Tragically, during his routine collection of protection money from a roadside vendor, Anand fell victim to a gunshot wound to his chest, perpetrated by a sharpshooter who swiftly vanished into the bustling marketplace. Anand was immediately rushed to the hospital. The main artery to his heart was ruptured, and Anand succumbed to his injuries upon arrival, his life cut short. In the aftermath, a relentless pursuit ensued, culminating in the apprehension and subsequent elimination of the shooter by the mafia syndicate. Concurrently, preparations pressed forward for Veena's impending nuptials. On the appointed day, Anand's remains were transported from Bombay to Mangalore via Air India, and then carried by van to his native village. Veena wanted to pay respect and visit Anand's house before the last rites. By that time, news had spread about how Anand had died, and everyone in the village knew of Anand being an employee of a gangster in Bombay. Veena's father reprimanded Veena and barred her from visiting Anand's house to pay her respects. Her in-laws also were against her visiting his house as it would be a bad omen to visit their place on the auspicious day of their wedding. Despite objections from her father and in-laws, her husband Arvind, displaying understanding and compassion, encouraged her to pay her respects. Overcoming familial resistance, Veena tearfully paid her final respects, finding solace in the opportunity to bid adieu to her uncle before his departure.

Thus, amidst the complexities of life's events, Veena found a semblance of closure, acknowledging the enigmatic ways of destiny.

- o 0 o -

STEP BROTHER

Shirur a small village was home to the head master of local secondary school. Mr. Nagarjun, residing with him was his wife Suma, his daughter Malati, and his son Varun. Their dwelling was an ancestral house with an adjoining plot of land. Malati's husband Narayan was selected as a police inspector in a nearby village. Narayan often returned on weekends. So Malati was permanently residing with her parents. Varun after his 8th standard wants to study further. But there was no high school. So when a post fell vacant in Narayana's police station, Varun got selected as a Police which irritated his father. But he was helpless.

Their life was relatively comfortable after Nagarjun's retirement. However, he found himself increasingly bored. Most of his time was spent in doing small work for the house or in the garden or sleeping. Slowly his health deteriorated and one fine morning his wife found him dead in his sleep.

Varun closed the ancestral house found a house on rent near the place of work and shifted there. So all three of them were happy. Many proposals came for Varun. Narayan choose one girl, whose father was a rich man, acres of land and the head priest of a temple in a nearby village. But there was a hitch. The girl was short, dark and plump. But her father was prepared to give lot of jewelry and cash. In those days, nobody considered education, or look of the girl. Family and position in society was the main criteria for an alliance. So Narayan finalised the marriage deal without consulting Varun. Hearing this, Varun was very upset. But he was not in a position to oppose his brother-in-law.

Marriage was solemnized with grandeur and Varun got a fat dowry. Varun was a very intelligent and meticulous person. He deposited all the cash in a bank which fetched him good interest. However, the bride Ratna was not a suitable match for Varun's good looks and charming personality.

Malati observing this match worked to maintain harmony in the house. One day she noticed Ratna experiencing morning sickness, leading her to suspect pregnancy. As time passed Ratna's condition progressed without any significant issues. The usual 7 months passed. Then Ratna was sent to her mother's place for delivery, after performing a small ceremony called Baby shower. Ratna went to her mother's place with much enthusiasm. There the baby shower was done in a grand way. Ratna's father Viswajit was a good man. But he had a weakness for gambling and he was a habitual gambler.

When on one Sunday, after the Puja was over Viswajit called Ratna and asked her to give some of her ornaments. Her mother cautioned her against this. So scared was Ratna of her father. She immediately gave few of her ornaments to her father. He lost all of it in betting Matka. Again the same pattern was repeated. She gave some more of her jewelry which was squandered in gambling. She was left helpless against her father's gambling habit. Ratna gave birth to a healthy boy. He inherited his father's good looks and mixtures of both, little short.

After a few months Ratna's father Viswajit sent word to Varun to take back his wife and son. Mr. Varun was waiting for the day. He immediately hired a cab and went to his father-in-law's house. On seeing Ratna without all her ornaments, Varun asked her "Whathappened to all your ornaments? Put them all it looks nice."

Ratna was so scared. She blurted out the truth. This ensured a quarrel between Viswajit and Varun.

Mr. Viswajit said "The ornaments were given to Ratna by me. I will return them after a few days. You take Ratna and the baby now". "No she cannot accompany me without her ornaments. I know you are a gambler. So I am leaving now without them you bring them to my house after getting all her ornaments. After the altercation Varun left in anger without his family.

Malati saw Varun returning without Ratna and the child she was shocked. She was helpless and shed silent tears.

The rift between Viswajit and Varun widened and Narayan riddled with guilt deteriorated in health and passed away. Varun despite his struggles eventually became the Police Inspector in place of his brother in law. He earned the trust of the villagers. Malati began grappling with Alzheimer's disease, while Varun provided her unwavering support.

Another six months passed. Mr. Varun had to go to Madras for some work related to his village Survey. On his way back he went to Mysore to see a drama. He was very much interested in dramas and Yakshagana. One drama called "Satya Harishchandra became very famous. Rani Taramati was enacted by a girl, fair, beautiful and elegant. Varun was bewitched by her beauty and elegance. Then he returned to his village.

After returning to his village Varun could not remove the memory of that girl from his mind. He started making enquiries about her. It also happened after much search he found out, that she is from a nearby village and her father is a drunkard. The girl became an obsession with him. He wanted to marry her.

In the meantime the drama company closed operations, because of bankruptcy. The two girls Saraswati and her cousin Suma came back to their village.

Varun wanted to marry Saraswati. Everybody advised him against it. He is still married to Ratna and he had a baby boy. It is illegal to marry again. But Varun was obsessed with Saraswati. So he mustered all his courage and went to meet her father. Her father was a drunkard and prepared to give her to any person, the highest bidder who pays a lot of money for his drunken spree. Varun withdrew half of his savings from the bank and went to meet her father. The deal was done. Saraswati was fed up of her father's drunken dramas. She saw Varun. He seems to be fairly well behaved and good looking with a steady job. She willingly followed him. So their life's journey started.

He brought her to his house. His sister got stunned!Such a beauty and decent looking girl! The girl was looking nervous. She was not knowing, what sort of reception she will get in his family. Malati told her brother "Take her back to her father. You will get only trouble and nothing else. Ratna's father is a influential person.

"No, I will never return her to her drunkard father. She followed me with full faith. I will not betray her faith. The sister kept quiet. Next day he called his family priest and they got married quietly in the house.

Saraswati was fed up of her father's drunken drama. So she adjusted to her present hardship and hot temper of her mentor.

Varun was a smart fellow and was getting good income from the villagers. He was staying in a rented house. There he got four children. 3 boys and a girl. He consort Saraswati became the unofficial wife, she was a sweet natured person.

After few years, Varun took a big plot of land from Govt. quota and built a big house. He was a garden lover. He brought many varieties of fruit trees from various parts of India and planted in his plot. It was a virgin land. Within a few years he got many varieties of fruits from his land. He got three more children, 2 girls and one boy in this house. Varun never bothered to enquire about his 1st wife and son.

Now his eldest son Vishwa completed his 8th standard. He was interested in further studies. So he was sent to a nearby city for higher education. Varun's son from Saraswati, Vishwa was a brilliant boy.

When he was in his final year in high school, Vishwa met his step brother in a dramatic way. They were all playing football. One boy fell and got hurt. All the boys rushed to his side. His name was Surya. Some instincts made Vishwa to be friends with the boy. Slowly he came to know the boy was his step brother. Surya was staying in his mother's sister's house. Surya told Vishwa his mother was abandoned by her husband and he was raised by his grandparents. Last year his mother died from Pneumonia. There was no High School in their village. So he was sent to a nearby town for high school education. He was staying with his mother's sister in town. After discreet enquiries Vishwa came to know Surya was his step brother. Then he had a open talk with Surya and the fact proved correct.

Summer holidays were approaching. Vishwa told Surya all about the truth and asked him to accompany him to meet his father. Surya was hesitant but ultimately curiosity got better of him.

When he went to Vishwa's house, he was shocked to see his father. His father was tall, fair and handsome and his step-mother at fifty, still a beauty. He could not but compare her to his own mother who was dark, short and ugly. He could realize his father's dilemma and why he abandoned her.

His father embraced him while tears flowing down his cheeks. All the siblings met and hugged him one by one. His step mother just patted him on his back. So it was an emotional reunion. Holidays were over without realizing it. Vishwa was in the final year of his high school, i.e. Matriculation. As soon as his results were out Vishwa went to Bombay in search of a job. But Surya's trip to his father's place continued. One year went very fast. Surya completed his Matric and went to Bangalore where his maternal uncle resided, to get a job. He got a job in a foreign bank, a plum job in those days.

Once Surya was in Bangalore, he forgot his father and the other family. Sometimes Vishwa used to write to him but he was busy with his own life. During one of their community meetings Surya met Ruchi, a girl vivacious, good looking and of kind nature. So Surya got fully immersed in his own affairs.

After a courtship of one year he married Ruchi the only people from his mother's side attended the marriage. He sent an invitation to his father and his other family but none came. After some more years, he heard the news that his father after retirement had a paralytic attack. Though Surya was a kind person he had not much affection for his father and the other family. He kept Vishwa in high esteem. Financially, he never wanted to help them. Then came the news that they all shifted to Bombay to Vishwa's house. Then he was busy with his own family with the addition of a boy and a girl. Though he was cordial to his father and the other family, he never forgets and forgave them for all the neglect and suffering caused to him and his mother.

- o 0 o -

THE FOREIGN CRAZE

Mr. Shekhar was running very fast to catch this long distance train to Bombay. A girl Gouri was also running behind him. Just in nick of time, he grabbed the train door handle and threw his bag and stood near the door. The train slowly caught momentum. He stood in the doorway and extended his hand for the girls support. The girl hesitated for a second, then gripped his hand firmly and boarded the train.

It was an A/C sleeper coach. People were all seated on the down seat. Shekhar and Gouri found some space and settled themselves on the seat. Shekhar after completely settling himself in his seat looked at the girl. She was, may be of his age or little younger than himself.

She wore a beige colour T- shirt and black jeans, her pony tail tied high up. She had chiseled features, tall and fair. It was love at first sight for Shekhar. The girl seemed little shy and looked at Shekhar from the corner of her eye.

Shekhar introduced himself "I am Shekhar from Belgaon, I am going to Bombay to appear for my medical entrance exam. He extended his hand towards Gouri, which she took without looking at him. "I am Gouri, from a village near Dharwad. I am also appearing for the same exam. Thanks for your timely support without which I would have missed the train. She withdraw her hand which Shekhar was still holding.

It was nearing 10 P.M. Some passengers in the compartment already started preparing for their night journey. Gouri got the lower birth and Shekhar got the upper birth. Gouri was still apprehensive about strangers. But she could feel secure about Shekhar. She had seen honesty in his eyes. He looked so decent. So both of them started chatting in a low voice so that the other passengers would not get disturbed. The next day at about 6 A.M. the train halted at Dadar station. Both got down with their bags and exchanged phone numbers and hoping to meet at the exam centre two days later.

Shekhar and Gouri met in the examination centre. Both were busy for the next three hours with their respective papers. The exam was conducted in two sessions. One in the morning and on in the evening. During lunch break both of them went to a nearby restaurant and had Thalis. This was the beginning of a long friendship that lasted several years.

After the exam, there was a gap of one week and the results were to be posted on the notice board of the same hall. Both of them passed with good marks.

Gouri decided to stay with her maternal aunt in Dadar and Shekhar stayed in the hospital's hostel. They both were posted in Sion Hospital.

Shekhar was of medium height, wheatish and good looking. Gouri was considered a beauty. They were as if made for each other.

Almost every day they used to meet in the evenings after the sessions were over. They used to visit all the tourist spots in Bombay. Chowpatty was their favourite haunt. Holidays were spent together. Lunch in some restaurant and a movie afterwards.

Though they never professed their love to each other, they were already known as a couple.

Both of them completed their M.B.B.S. and the internship of 1 ½ years, started. The internship was in a rural area. They both were posted in a village in Vasai Taluka. They hired two rooms in a building. They used to prepare breakfast either in Gouri's room or Shekhar's. room lunch and dinner was delivered by one family. So life was smooth and without any hassles 1 ½ years passed in a jiffy.

After returning to Bombay, they have to select their respective subject for post graduation. Shekhar choose Orthopedic and Gouri General Medicine.

Gouri knew Shekhar's life ambition was to go to America and make lot of money. They were in the final year of post graduation, Gouri got a telegram, she had to go to her native place on an emergency basis. Her father was seriously ill. Gouri could not meet Shekhar before she left Bombay she kept a note for Shekhar and left without meeting him. There was no medical facility in their village. Her father was a heart patient. His family wanted to take him to either Bombay or Bangalore. But after he met Gouri, his condition worsened. He made her promise that she will serve the poor people of the village, setting up a nursing home there. He breathed his last holding her hands. After the 13th day was over, Gouri returned to Bombay and to her studies.

After returning from native place Gouri was very quiet and avoided meeting Shekhar. One evening Shekhar met Gouri in the corridor of the hospital, Shekhar got hold of her hand, pulled her to a corner and asked her "Gouri what is the matter, why are you avoiding me ?".

"You are hurting me Shekhar" cried Gouri. Then only Shekhar realised the intensity of his grip on her hand. He immediately let go of her hand and said "I am extremely sorry".

He earnestly asked her "you cannot ignore me like this. I have the right to know the reason behind your silence.

"We will meet at Guru kripa Restaurant in the evening. I will explain to you everything, said Gouri with all sincerity. "That is like my nice girl" Shekhar smiled at her, Gouri also smiled back.

Shekhar and Gouri met in the hotel in the evening. Gouri was more relaxed and explained to him the circumstances under which she had to take the drastic step. "Now we are at different poles. Neither you can change your plans of going to U.S.A. nor can I forget the promise given to my father on his death bed and in the present circumstances we cannot continue our friendship which will have no meaning. So we should make efforts to keep distance between ourselves. Gouri was morally an upright girl. Shekhar was touched by Gouri's sincereity. He took Gouri's hand in his hand and told her in a soft tone "Gouri, I love you, I will abide by whatever decision you take, that will be OK with me". I cannot abandon the idea of my going to U.S.A. and settling there. In course of time, I may marry another girl, but my heart always belongs to you".

Tears started rolling down Gouri's cheek; Shekhar took his handkerchief and wiped her tears. They parted after hugging each other. Shekhar sat for some more time, to control his emotion. Then he also started to go to the hospital.

Many years passed, Gouri never married. One day Gouri saw a couple on the Facebook with two kids a boy and a girl Shekhar used to share his family photographs on Facebook. Gouri in return posted the photograph and news of the nursing home on Facebook.

Shekhar after migrating to U.S.A. did a further course in Urology and had a clinic with an American doctor as a partner. He made lot of money.

One day Gouri got a donation of Rs.10,00,000/-. She immediately knew it is from Shekhar. Immediately she posted a "Thank you" message. Gouri was married to her Nursing Home. She considered it her family. Shekhar gesture brought tears in her eye. Sometimes Gouri felt the absence of children in her life. But life is fulfilling in different ways.

- o 0 o -

ABSOLUTE POWER

Sulakshana was a vivacious girl, tall, slim and beautiful. Her father was a temple Pujari. She wanted to study and become a Lawyer. So her father found a lawyer with lot of dowry, a lawyer as a groom. Sulakshana had a liking for music. She told her husband she wanted to pursue music. He arranged a music teacher for her. Within a few years, she became an expert In the music. The teacher was also amazed at her learning capacity. She started giving tuition to students. Her name spread far and wide. She was happy, basking in her glory. They were residing in Chennai.

One day the local regiment in charge of the military was passing near their house, he heard her singing. The music touched his heart. One day he sent his soldiers to fetch her to listen to the music for some time.

After discussing the issue with her husband she went along with the accompanying soldiers to the campus. She sang for a short time and she came back with lot of presents and in a military van with full honours. This went on for about two months. In the meantime, the young Colonel was attracted towards Sulakshana.

One evening Sulakshana after returning from the temple was abducted by a bunch of hooligans. There was no news of her for about 10 days. On the 10th day, she was dropped near the temple vicinity by the same hooligans. They were not natives of Chennai. The whole drama was orchestrated by the Captain. Sulakshana in spite of repeated request by the family members did not utter a word. She was crying continuously. Her husband suspected some foul play. But he was very earnest and gave full support to his wife. Many days passed, slowly they all forget the incident. But Sulakshana a vivacious girl become morose and sad. She lost interest in everything. She stopped tuitions. Slowly she became a skeleton. In the meantime, she became pregnant. Her husband suspected some sort of foul play in her ordeal. Sulakshana never utter a word. The mention of the hushup gave her fits. So each and every member of the house was careful not to mention about it. But when the baby was born, it was very fair and its eyes with a tingle of bluer. Her husband was the first to notice it. Sulkshana refuse to feed the baby, and was averse to any contact with the baby. Her husband correctly surmised that the baby was not his. But he had not got the guts to talk to Sulakshana about those dark 10 days Sulakshana said she was kept in a dark room and tortured by some native people. There was no motive behind it. But time and tide waits for nobody, time was going rapidly. Sulakshana baby started going to school. In the midst of all this catastrophe Mr. Venu Sulakshana's husband shifted to Bangalore. For some time life was peaceful. Venu her husband practicing in Bangalore. It took time to the practice to be picked up. But he was a very patient man. Slowly, the business progressed. Roopa Sulakshana's daughter wanted to learn Bharatnatyam. Her father was against this, but Sulakshana encouraged her. Roopa was tall, very fair with a shade of blue in her eyes. Her co-students always teased her about her eyes. She got hurt. Many a times, she thought if she can get operated and remove the blue tinge from her eyes.

Roopa was a Bharatnatyam dancer. Once during the annual school day, she performed a dance performance and a film producer noticed her dance. He sent an offer for her to act in his dance drama called Dushyant Shakuntala. Roopa was selected and the Drama became very successful. Afterwards offers started pouring from Bollywood. Roopa shifted to Bombay. She got many offers from Bollywood. She was very careful. Her mother always accompanied her. Even on outdoor shootings.

Roopa was in love with a producer director a married man with children. Her mother was unaware of this fact. Two or three months passed, Roopa's mother noticed the condition of her daughter. History repeats itself. Sulakshana was so scared of the situation. She started getting fits. Her fast is repeating again. She told her daughter to get abortion done immediately. No repeat of the past. Her manager Mr. Harish whois in know of everything revealed to her friend Satish. Satish was Roopa's childhood friend. Recently Satish was a real estate Agent and doing very well. He immediately rushed to Bombay. He was very sympathetic with her. Her mother also liked Satish. So a hush-hush marriagewas arranged.

She continued her dancing career along with her film career. An abortion was done before the marriage. Satish knew everything. After a few pictures, she shifted to Bangalore to pursue her dance career. She opened a dance academy and started teaching the children Bharatnatyam. For a long time, her mother till her death guided her in her affairs. Roopa got a son andhe also pursued Bharatnatyam. Roopa lived upto a ripe age and practiced her passion Bharatnatyam.

- o 0 o -

FAMILY PRESTIGE

They had a crackling chemistry. Sangita and Arjun were in love. Arjun finally agreed to approach his parents for their approval for their marriage. They both were students in the MBA section of Bajaj Institute of Management Studies.

Sangita hailed from a well-known family of Bombay originally from Kerala. The family was cultural, philanthropist and one of the well-known families of Mumbai.

Sangita was intelligent, good in sports and very charming. Arjun was a sports person. You cannot call him handsome, aristocratic look, his hair little greying at the temples, of moderate height. The aristocratic stance was because of his attitude or his lineage still a debatable question.

Arjun was the eldest son of his wealthy parents having coffee plantations in Coorg. His father's brother Venu also was a joint owner of the plantation.

After the demise of their father, both brothers decided to stay separately.

But all the festivals and religious ceremonies were celebrated in their ancestral house. Each one will go with their immediate family to the main house, attend the Puja, have a sumptuous meal prepared by the cooks, the daughter-in-laws would come and get an opportunity to display their sarees and diamond jewellery.

The grand old lady the mother of the two brothers stayed in the old house with a retinue of maids. On one such occasion Arjun raised the question of his marriage with his father. The grandmother was the first one to veto the proposal and then both brothers conferred and outright rejected the proposal. They said a girl from outside their circle, will not suit their prestige and they had to stop this trend of boys selecting girls other than the established industrial families of Coorg. Arjun wanted to tell something, but his father made a sign to silence him. Arjun kept quiet but on reaching home he reacted sharply for silencing him. He is not a small boy. He is an adult and he had all the right to put his point of view.

He told his father, they were no more an established business family nor they are from a royal lineage. The truth hit his father very hard. But recovering fast he told his son to choose between the family and the girl. Arjun was very upset. He returned to Bombay and to his studies. He met Sangita and they had a long discussion about his family and their views and they decided to end their friendship on a cordial note.

In between Sangita's parents were in Coorg for one of their friends son's wedding. They thought it, god send opportunity to meet Arjun parents. They phoned them and went to meet them. They were very upset over the reception they got in Arjun's place. Arjun's father did not come out of the room. His mother made an attempt to have some conversation. It was the month of April very hot. They did not offer them any refreshment. Not even a glass of water. They were disgruntled with the treatment meted out to them and returned vowing, never to have anything with the family. Sangita's father was an engineer in a reputed firm, her mother a headmistress of a school.

When they returned to Bombay they told their daughter, they will never consent to her marriage to Arjun. So the fate was sealed. After returning from Coorg Arjun met Sangita and explained to her his family's decision. Sangita was understanding, she realised their further friendship will not bring any happiness to either of them or to the family.

That was the final year of their course. After college, they both lost contact. Sangita got a job in New Zealand. There she met a simple M.B.A. boy from Bangalore. After a formal courtship they got married. She had an adoring husband, a loving mother-in-law and their family completed with a daughter and a son. She had the resilience and practicability of a sensible girl.

She heard news from common friends, Arjun got married to a girl from a Kerala industrial family. Sangita met Arjun during an annual health check-up in Breach Candy Hospital after many years. Sangita saw Arjun with his wife and a mentally retarded son. Sangita felt sad for Arjun.

When they came face to face at the cash counter Arjun said a feeble "Hai". There was regret written all over his face. He felt defeated in life. On the contrary Sangita looked happy and exorbitant.

It was Arjun's family, the main cause for his suffering. He remembered the good old days when he and Sangita were in love and happy. His life has been devastated by the false prestige and ambition of his family. Sudden meeting with Sangita flooded his memory with the happy times they spent together. He realised whatever happened is destiny which he cannot reverse.

He hated his father and his family. They were the main culprits for his suffering. Then he thought of his understanding wife and his helpless son whom he cannot abandon.

Arjun realised his family was wallowing in their age old customs and belief and that put a seal on Arjun's and Sangita's friendship.

Then he realised destiny plays a hand in all our relationships which we cannot overrule.

- o 0 o -